The Curious Childhood of Patty O.

Growing up in White Bear Lake, Minnesota

The Curious Childhood of Patty O.

Growing up in White Bear Lake, Minnesota

By Pat Olchefski-Winston

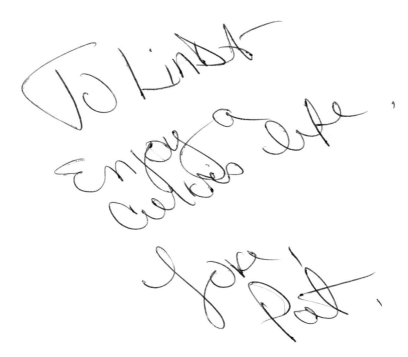

ISBN 978-1-105835-025

Dedication

Mom, this one's for you! Love, Patty

"There either is or is not, that's the way things are. The colour of the day. The way it felt to be a child. The saltwater on your sunburnt legs. Sometimes the water is yellow, sometimes it's red. But what colour it may be in memory, depends on the day. I'm not going to tell you the story the way it happened. I'm going to tell it the way I remember it."
— Charles Dickens, *Great Expectations*

"What is to give light must endure burning."
—Victor E. Frankl

Table of Contents

Preface

This, my first book, started as a collage of bits and pieces of stories, most completely true and some fictionalized, that I recalled about my childhood growing up in White Bear Lake, Minnesota. After being away from my hometown for many years, I began to miss its quaint charm and the colorful characters who had filled my curious life during the '60s and early '70s. I started jotting down my favorite memories of special moments shared with my family, friends, and the various townspeople I grew up around. Here are my stories. Most of the names have been changed to protect the innocent and the not so … but indeed, the place is real.

The painting on the cover and the others in the book are recent watercolors from my latest trips back home. Being an artist/painter has been my main profession for the last thirty years. My artwork can be seen and purchased on my website: www.olchefski.com.

Acknowledgements

Thanks go to my wonderful editor, Christine Susany, for her professional experience and literary expertise that was much needed to transform my raw material into a publishable manuscript, and to my talented soul sister copyeditor, Susan Walker, for her amazing abilities to understand and finalize my stories for print. Your support throughout this adventure is much appreciated.

Thanks also to my husband, my immediate and extended family, and all my glorious and uplifting friends who continually urged me on. You inspired and believed in me, knowing that writing was a new kind of art form for me to attempt. You are all the best!

PART ONE
IN THE BEGINNING

His Name Was Nick

I never knew my father. Mom said he was a *"no-good son-of-a-bitch"* and wouldn't let him have anything to do with me. Wouldn't even put his name on my birth certificate as father! She said he didn't deserve it.

As a child, I never did know what he had done to warrant my mother's wrath because no one in her presence would ever talk about it. If his name came up, Mom would explode in a string of expletives that would make any sailor blush. Grandma would say, "Ruby, you shouldn't speak such words in front of the children," and then Mom would tell Grandma to get the hell out of her life. Meanwhile, Grandpa would just chuckle at Mom's outbursts and mutter, "She calls 'em as she sees 'em."

Still, this shadow man I never knew would be allowed to take my brothers away for weekend visits, "if and when he's sober," Mom stipulated, which times were few and far between as best as I can recall. When he came to collect "his boys," I remember watching out the window and wondering about that man behind the wheel who was, but was not, a part of my life. I had tears, some only on the inside, and some openly flowing down my cheeks.

Mom's Little Hand

I never noticed that my mom had only one normal hand—that is, a hand with five fully formed fingers—until I was about ten years old. I never noticed because she could do anything any other mom could do, sometimes even better. I never noticed that she was different. I never noticed her "deformity" until the day her partial little left hand patted my knee. I guess people now would call that a mother/daughter moment. She smiled down at me and said, "'Don't be so shy, little one. You are my shining star."

I don't remember having felt sad, or crying, or acting funny, and yet she felt like saying these words to me that day. It was then I looked, for the first time it seemed, at her miniature left hand. I held it up to my face as she rubbed my cheeks with it, and I saw that this hand had no fingers—just tiny stumps where her fingers should have been—and it was about one-third the size of her other hand. Suddenly, I got teary-eyed and looked deep into her cloudy, blue eyes. Instinctively, she knew what I had finally noticed. She smiled and said, "Honey, I was born this way. Don't think for a second that it stops me from doing anything."

That moment was memorable for both of us. To me, Mom's little hand was as soft, cute, and smooth as any hand I had ever touched. What's more, I thought, she didn't have to worry about her fingernails growing too long or getting dirt underneath them. To me, her hand was perfect. From that moment on, my favorite thing about my mom was her special, God-given hand. As far as I knew, it was the only one like it in the whole world, and I loved her even more for that. This special hand made her unique and, in my eyes, the most beautiful person I had ever seen.

I never thought of Mom's little hand as an abnormality, and I hated when people stared, glared, or stopped to ask about it when they were supposed to just keep walking. As far as I was concerned, this "incomplete" hand made my mom the most complete person and best mom ever. With this hand, she could hold and balance pots and pans, fill coffee cups and cereal bowls, cuddle kittens and babies, and tote things big and small. Oh, and she could also drive a car without any problem and even ride bikes with me. Yet, even though she could do and manage anything with this hand while at home, she was always shy about displaying it in public and often put it in her pocket to keep people from gawking. I guess it was easier for her that way.

Because I grew up with a special mom, I tended to be drawn to other people with so-called deformities. It seems I was born with a sixth sense that these people are perfect in their own way. The fact that all these people were put on this earth looking a little bit different made them special in my eyes. I grew up believing they were God's favorite people because they lived their lives in a league of their own—each blessed with a uniqueness that set them apart from the mainstream and, too often, boring folks. To this day, I go out of my way to talk with and be nice to those among us whom some choose to label as "special needs" while labeling themselves as "normal."

Less than Perfect

What I loved most about my mom was her special hand. Mom's left hand was just a third the size of her right one, and it had only rounded stumps for fingers. To me, her hand was a small detail, but according to Mom, Grandma considered this less-than-perfect hand to be a cause for rejection. I always believed mothers were supposed to love their children and treat them with sweetness and kindness no matter what, but Mom said that wasn't the case with Grandma. From the stories Mom told, Grandma was mean to her from the day Mom was born.

That day should have been a super-duper happy day for Grandma. Three minutes before Mom came out, a boy was born. Mom always called him her "twin who came three minutes earlier," as if that made any difference in my young mind. However, it evidently made a big difference to her and Grandma. This baby appeared close to perfect and complete. He had all of his fingers and toes, and Grandma was overjoyed with him at first glance. She named him Roy Lee. We kids always just called him Uncle Roy.

Now, I'm sure Mom was just as beautiful and sweet a baby as Uncle Roy was, except for one thing—her less-than-perfect hand. I would have expected Grandma to be grateful about having two babies at once instead of just one like when her first fatty, bratty child, Jenny Lou, was born; but, according to Mom, when Grandma saw her new baby girl with the shriveled up stub for a left arm, she was disappointed about giving birth to a deformed daughter. Mom said Grandma had rejected her right from the start. While she continued to treat Uncle Roy special and give him lots of love and attention, Grandma treated Mom with indifference. At best, Grandma ignored her altogether; at worst, she treated her badly. Mom often said that cruelty was Grandma's main character flaw.

Mom survived those early years of rejection. She had no choice. She survived by being strong-willed, determined, and, most of all, beautiful inside and out.

Luckily for Grandma, Mom was the forgiving type. When Grandma got old and broken down, she needed Mom. It seemed to me that when people got old, they also got soft and weak in their bones, so they were willing to accept help from anyone. In Grandma's case, she would even accept help from the deformed daughter she had treated so badly all her life. Mom did everything in her power to feel and show forgiveness toward Grandma in her old age, which was more than Grandma had ever done for Mom.

One day, Mom took Grandma into the woods to pick fresh berries. Then she helped her clean them and served them to her for lunch, covered with fresh cream. Mom said that treat had made Grandma so happy that she had sent the extra berries home to share with us kids.

Grandma died a tired, old woman at the age of ninety-six. She had been mean to Mom all her life, and she had never said she was sorry. I asked Mom if Grandma had gone to heaven. Mom said, "Maybe. She was half-good and half-bad, just like the rest of us. I think God probably had a place for her."

I often wondered whether Grandma ever realized that she was a less-than-perfect person, too.

Grandpa's Tricks and Treats

Grandpa had to be one of the funniest people ever. I remember times when he'd emerge from his bedroom in his low-slung trousers held up by faded red suspenders that draped across the paper-thin T-shirt clinging to his shoulders; he'd lumber down the long hallway to the living room like an awakening alien from outer space. My brothers and I could always tell when he was up to something because his silly grin gave him away every time. He'd approach us with pure mischief glimmering in his eyes and then proceed to chase us all over the house, out the back door, and all around the yard before Grandma would scream, "*Husband!*" That would end the chase, but my brothers and I would end up rolling around in the grass, laughing our heads off.

Another time, Grandpa said, "Come here, children. Come shake my hand." He was seated in one of the overstuffed chairs in Grandma's tastefully decorated living room. We gathered around him, and my oldest brother, Mel, was the first to shake Grandpa's hand.

"Ouch! What was that?" Mel yelled as he jumped back and pulled his hand away from Grandpa's.

Grandpa just chuckled. "You're next, Johnny. Come shake Grandpa's hand."

Johnny, afraid of what was in Grandpa's hand, was already running out of the room, but Mel collared him before he could make a clean break. "Okay, Grandpa," Johnny said, dreading what was waiting for him. Fearfully, he grasped Grandpa's hand and then blurted out, "Ouch! That hurt!" with a sense of shock and pain.

By this time, Grandpa was laughing hysterically. "Okay, Patty, it's your turn," he said. "Come on and shake my hand." Bravely, I put my hand in his and felt a tiny pin prick my palm. Without saying a word, I looked up and saw his smiling eyes and corny grin. Grandpa said, "Look, kids. It's a trick. When I press down on this white button, a tiny pin pricks you. Want to try it?" After seeing how little this hidden gadget was, we understood that he was just being a prankster once again.

Pulling pranks was Grandpa's way of showing his love for us, and Grandpa was full of pranks. Thankfully, most didn't hurt like the handshake trick, but some were just as scary. One night, he came out of his bedroom wearing the ugliest plastic monster mask imaginable. He had the mask pulled way down over his head and came walking down the hall hunched over like Frankenstein and growling like a vampire wolf. We all ran for a door to get away from this fierce yet funny-looking monster. While Johnny and I made our escape through the patio door, Mel charged through the front door; but we could all hear Grandpa laughing behind us as we ran. After Grandpa scared us a dozen times with a different mask each time, we finally gave up running and instead laughed 'til our sides hurt at how silly Grandpa could be. Grandpa was funny; Grandpa was fat; and we all loved him very much, especially me.

I loved Grandpa even when I was uncertain about his actions. I remember one time arriving at Grandma and Grandpa's house and walking up the driveway toward the front door. There was Grandpa lying flat on his back, sound asleep, in the middle of the grassy front lawn. The sun was straight up in the summer sky, and while serving us kids iced tea and freshly baked cookies, I overheard Mom whispering to Grandma. "Dad's drunk, again," she said. "Can't you tell him not to drink so much when he knows we're coming to visit?"

Grandma shrugged her shoulders and sighed. "Ruby, I have no control over his drinking. He keeps his booze hidden in his shed. He thinks I don't know about it. Hell, I've known for years what he's up to when he goes out there to 'work on his hobby.' He's not building bird feeders. He's drinking. At least it keeps him out of the house and out of my hair. As long as he stays out there, he doesn't bother me."

I was shocked. Grandpa was passed out drunk, not just napping. Still, it didn't change the fact that I loved him. Grandpa was always kind and sweet to me, drunk or not.

Sometimes, when Grandma was extra busy cooking up something special, we got to share some afternoon adventures with Grandpa. To get us out of Grandma's house (and her hair), Grandpa, with courtly generosity, would pile us kids into his pickup and drive south along the St. Croix to Afton, another beautiful river town. Afton boasted several colorful shops and stores, but the one we all looked forward to visiting was Thelma's Ice Cream Parlor on Main Street. Next door to the ice cream shop was Lerk's Saloon, a place Grandpa liked to "pop into" for a drink or two whenever possible. Across the street was a huge city park with all kinds of swings and things to play on, very convenient for us kids.

When we got to town, Grandpa would dutifully accompany us into Thelma's and set us up on the counter stools. "What flavor floats your boats today?" he'd ask.

"Do they have butter pecan?" I'd ask.

11

"Of course they have butter pecan, Sweetie. What would you like, Johnny?"

"Vanilla with chocolate syrup, please," Johnny would answer.

"And you, Mel?"

"I want strawberry. Two scoops."

"Okay. Two scoops it is."

We'd all be seated at the counter contentedly devouring Grandpa's special treat when he would say, "Children, I need to pop in next door to visit with Lerk. I'll be back in half an hour. When you finish your ice cream or get bored, Mel, take your brother and sister across the street to the playground. I'll meet you there."

After we'd finish our ice cream, Mel would lead us across the street to the park. Johnny and I would play on the swings, pushing each other around and around on the merry-go-round and climbing up and slid down the very long, twisting sliding board at least a half-dozen times before Grandpa would call to us from outside the saloon, "Come on, kids. Time to go."

Mel once again would help us cross the street, even though there were very few cars around by then. Grandpa would load us into his pickup, and we'd all head for home. It would have been a fun day. We had shared a great outing with Grandpa and, as far as I was concerned, all was right in my world. Afternoons spent with Grandpa were the best of times.

Learning to Swim and Sew

Grandma and Grandpa lived in a lovely village south of Stillwater called St. Croix Beach. There, the river runs wild, and the swimming is grand. Some of my most memorable weekends were spent at my grandparents' home located on the banks of the St. Croix River, an upper tributary of the mighty Mississippi. I loved going to their house because there were always plenty of fun things to do, especially during the summer when we could fish and play in the river. One day, Grandpa decided he would teach us how to swim. He said we needed to learn this important lesson because it might save our lives someday. "Besides, it's as easy as falling off a log," he said, leading us down the path to the riverbank.

"The first lesson you need to learn is how to float." I figured this must be important because Grandpa rarely spoke with such authority. "Watch how easy it is for me to float on my back," he said as he waded out into the deeper water. Now, Grandpa was a *big* man, tall and fat. No way is that hulk going to float, I thought as I watched him walk further out until, at last, he was standing in shoulder-high water. "Okay, kids, watch this!" he shouted, and we all watched with amazement as that huge man plopped onto his back, crossed his hands over his chest—with his ankles crossed too—and proceeded to float and bob around like an inflatable toy. It looked like magic. All we could see was his big head, whale belly, and winter-white toes sticking up out of the water. Could floating really be as simple as that? I wondered.

Then we heard him call out to us again. "I'll be back shortly," he hollered, and we watched him float downstream with the currents for what seemed like forever. Just when we were beginning to worry that we might never see him again, he flipped himself over and swam back to the dock like a young, skilled athlete. Climbing out of the water, only slightly out of breath, he approached us. "It's your turn now. I'll watch."

Johnny and Mel took turns trying to float like Grandpa, but they both failed. Finally, it was my turn. I walked out into the deeper water and did everything Grandpa had told me to do. I laid my head back into the water, lifted my legs until my body was straight, and then I relaxed. Immediately, I was floating, just like Grandpa. It was easy. The only thing I couldn't do at first was fold my arms onto my chest, so I just let them float all by themselves, sort of like propellers. My brothers sort of got the hang of it after several more attempts, but neither of them could ever float as well as Grandpa and I. They said it was because I was a girl and had more fat on my body, but I never did believe that explanation.

It turned out that Grandpa was not only good at floating; he was a strong swimmer, too. After that first floating lesson, Grandpa took us down to the river every time we visited and gave us another swimming lesson. By summer's end, we could all swim like pros. We knew the different strokes and how to stay safe in the water. After that summer, none of us ever feared getting caught in an eddy or a current of the mighty Mississippi, or any other body of water for that matter. Thanks to Grandpa.

*****

Grandma was different. She didn't care much for fun activities like swimming. She was all about what she called "the domestic arts"—sewing, cooking, and gardening. She was good at all of them, and lucky for me, she was willing to teach me her skills. Mom, who didn't receive any of Grandma's time or attention, hadn't been so lucky. But Grandma did teach my closest cousin, Mary Kay, and me how to sew one summer.

Mary Kay used to get dropped off at my grandparents' house for weeks at a time during the summer. During one of her extended visits, Grandma decided to treat the two of us to a shopping trip to the historic river town of Stillwater. I loved going to Stillwater! A lot of people, and I'm one of them, considered it to be one of the most beautiful places in the world. The streets were lined with quaint shops and restaurants, but Grandma shopped there because it had a wonderful fabric store. She said it had the best selection of materials in the state. So, that's where we were heading on this Saturday-afternoon adventure with Grandma.

When we arrived at the store, Grandma told us that we could each choose three yards of any cotton fabric to make a dress and she would teach us how to sew when we returned home. After looking at what seemed to be hundreds of bolts of multi-colored prints, I finally selected a light-purple floral pattern that reminded me of springtime lilac blossoms. Mary Kay's choice was a green-and-yellow plaid, but Grandma said, "Honey, not a plaid. It's too hard to match up the lines. Pick something—anything—else." Mary Kay looked disappointed until she found a really pretty orangey-pink cotton brocade. It was a little more expensive than the plaid, but Grandma said the price was within her allowance. So we gathered up our purchases and headed home to start our lessons.

The next day, with our fabrics, notions, and a simple dress patterns spread out on the dining room table, we were ready for our first sewing lesson. Grandma showed us how to pin the pattern to the fabric, how to size it, how to cut it, and how to thread and operate her Singer sewing machine. It took a lot of time to go through all the proper steps, but we kept at it for several hours. Mary Kay was a faster learner because I spent more time watching than doing. That's just my nature. I like to spend time observing first; doing always comes second. Unfortunately, I hadn't made much progress by the time Grandma came in and said, "Time for lunch. Let's heat up that potato soup and have a turkey sandwich. You both need a little break before you little ladies sew your fingers to the dress." She was right. We were both tired and hungry.

After lunch and a little walk outside, Mary Kay and I continued our sewing lesson with Grandma. Three hours later, we had something to show for all our hard work. Unfortunately, my dress hung on me like a sack. "Grandma," I said, disappointed, "I thought I measured it correctly. Look at me! This dress is way too big."

"Take it off, Patty, and I'll show you how to take it in," Grandma said. "It's much better to have it too big than too small. You can fix it if it's too large, but not if it's too small and you've already cut away most of the fabric." After removing my dress, Grandma gave me my first lesson in alterations.

By early evening, right before dinner, our dresses were finished. They matched in style, but Mary Kay's fit her better. Grandma tried to reassure me by telling me that Mary Kay was easier to fit because she was a bit plumper. I'm not sure either of us believed her, but we were proud of our efforts. Mary Kay and I continued our sewing lessons with Grandma, and over the years, our sewing abilities continued to improve. We eventually began making all of our own school clothes—even through high school. I was really proud that I could create my own outfits and save money, too, all because of Grandma.

Hold the Rhubarb, Please!

Aside from teaching me how to be an accomplished sewer, Grandma also taught me to love flowers and to garden. She could grow anything, and did, even Lady's Slippers—flowers she said we should never touch. They were beautiful but poisonous. If we touched them, she said, we would get the worst rash of our lives. I never attempted to go near them. No one did. Grandma had warned us, and we believed her. However, I often wondered how she could work with those flowers if she could not touch them. Then I saw her yard gloves. They weren't like any gloves I had ever seen. These special gloves made of thick leather protected her perfect hands from the stickers, bugs, and poisonous plants that grew in her garden.

Gardening was one of Grandma's favorite pastimes. Besides growing beautiful flowers, she also liked to grow her own vegetables. She would pick them when they were fresh to cook or "put them up" to use during the cold winter months when fresh vegetables were scarce and expensive.

Cooking and baking were Grandma's other talents (my favorites, too). She baked the best pies in the world, and she knew how to make taffy and other candies. Although sweet treats seemed to be her specialties, she could also cook up some great meals. She would use the vegetables she had harvested from her garden to make soups and stews and sauces, goulash and various hot dishes, along with meat pies, pot roasts, and, always, gravy. She wasn't a gourmet cook. She was just a damned good cook.

The only thing Grandma ever made that turned my stomach was her rhubarb pie. Grandma always looked forward to spring when the rhubarb that grew wild around her house would shoot up strong and sturdy stalks that she would cut down and chop up to make her prized rhubarb pies. One day, she served me a slice of rhubarb pie, and as she cut the pie, she told me that fresh rhubarb was a real treat that could only be enjoyed once a year. Expecting one of her sweet delights, I took one bite—and proceeded to vomit all over my plate.

Later, Mom and Grandma said that I must have been getting the flu, and it just happened to hit me when I took a bite of that pie. However, I said the pie was too sour, and it had turned my stomach. Mom said since it had taken me a week to get well, it couldn't have been the pie. I said it didn't matter; the pie tasted terrible. From that moment on, I've hated rhubarb, in pie or alone, and have never eaten it again.

Grandma and Grandpa

Grandma and Grandpa were as different as salt is from sugar, and I loved each of them for different reasons. Together, just like salt and sugar, they added taste and flavor to my life. While Grandma possessed the good taste, Grandpa provided my favorite lifetime flavors: fun and laughter.

I always thought Grandma was pretty, in an old-lady kind of way. Her skin was soft and smooth, and her hair wavy and gray. She loved beautiful clothes and decorated her home with unique and colorful art and objects collected on her many winter vacations. Grandpa, on the other hand, was a big man who had a round belly that hung over his belt and jowls that hung low on his neck. As hard as I tried, I could never imagine either of them as ever having been young and pretty or tall and handsome. They were just Grandma and Grandpa. For her part, Grandma never laughed much that I could remember. Although she was always kind to me and taught me many things, she was a strict and stern teacher. She didn't waste her time on frivolities. Meanwhile, Grandpa was full of tricks and treats, and never seemed to tire of entertaining us three rambunctious kids.

When Grandma spoke to Grandpa, she always called him *Husband.* She would say "Husband this" and "Husband that," unless or until she became really, really upset with him. Then she would scream his name at the top of her lungs, "*George!*" When she called him for meals, she would holler, "Husband—breakfast!" or "Husband—lunch!" or "Husband—dinner!" Grandma was bossy, so Grandpa came when he was called. He rarely talked during meals, but he'd often give us kids the silliest grin or smirk when he thought Grandma wasn't looking. He acted like a kid, and we loved it. If Grandma caught him, she'd get pretty irritated.

Grandpa would also irritate Grandma when he took his teeth out during meals. Instead of placing them in the little dish she set out for them, he'd set them on her fancy linen tablecloth. I still remember the hard stare she would give him as he continued to eat, ignoring her completely. However, the real clincher came the day Grandma served up our most favorite home-churned vanilla ice cream for dessert. She had scooped the ice cream into one of her daintiest dessert dishes, and while the rest of us gobbled it up lickety-split, Grandpa sat quietly, waiting for it to melt. Then, just as the rest of us finished licking our spoons, he picked up the bowl in both hands and drank the icy slush down in one big gulp. Grandma glared at him in total disbelief and horror, but never said a word. When she turned away, Grandpa winked at us and smiled. We giggled quietly, muffling our laughter behind our napkins. This was their life—much like a game of cat and mouse—but I guess they were happy with each other.

One thing that always intrigued me about my grandparents' house was the huge mural that took up the entire back wall of the dining room. I knew Grandma liked to travel and often took long vacations with her friends, but I had never given much thought about where she went on these trips. Finally, one day after sitting through another family dinner at Grandma's house, I asked her, "Grandma, what is that picture, and how is it stuck to your wall?"

"Patty," Grandma replied, "that's a photo of the Golden Gate Bridge in San Francisco. I had it framed and shipped back here after my last trip there. Do you like it?"

"Yes, Grandma. It's beautiful. Is the bridge really gold?" I asked.

"No, Patty. The bridge isn't gold, but it does glisten like gold in the sunset, and the entire city seems to shine with an indescribable brilliance. San Francisco is one of the most cultured and beautiful cities in the world."

I wasn't sure what she meant by cultured, but I had to agree after studying the photo that this surely had to be one of the most beautiful places I could ever imagine. "I want to go there someday, Grandma. I want to visit beautiful places, too, just like you."

"Oh, Sweetie Pie, I think you and I have the same travel bug inside us. If that's the case, I have no doubt you will experience your own adventures in faraway places someday."

I wasn't sure I understood what she meant when she spoke of travel bugs, personal adventures, and faraway places, but I did know that this was the first time I had ever heard my grandmother speak to me with the soft tones of affection and appreciation. Somehow, at that moment, I knew, too, that she had made an important prediction for my future life.

PART II
WELCOME TO WHITE BEAR LAKE

White Bear Lake: A Fine Place to Call Home

The summer before I entered the third grade, Mom said, "Get in the car, kids. We're moving to a new scenic resort town. It's not too far from here, and it's a really nice place because it has the most beautiful lake you will ever see. And the best part is Bruce found us a pretty corner house not far from the lake."

My older brother, Melvin (sometimes called Mel), didn't seem too happy about this unexpected news. "Mom, what about my friends here in Arden Hills?" he asked. "They want me to be the quarterback in the fall."

Mom, who was in one of her better moods that day, said, "Honey, don't you worry. You're so good at sports, I'm sure Sunrise

Junior High will want you as their quarterback too, and their school is supposed to be the best around. We need to go now. Get in the car, and I'll answer your questions later."

Mel may have been worried about his football career, but I was worried about everything—mostly because I was super shy and timid. Meeting new kids and making new friends was going to be hard. At least that's what I thought at the time. But, before I go on, I had better explain who Bruce was and how he came to be a part of our family.

A couple of years before we moved to White Bear Lake my mom, my brothers, and I were living in the little town of Snail Lake. One nice fall day, this big fat man with a huge round belly and a funky-smelling cigar clamped between the teeth of his rather large mouth came to visit Mom with a stack of Encyclopedia Britannica books—books that had everything anyone would ever need to know. I guess he was trying to sell them to her, but no way was that ever going to happen because we were close to dirt poor. This big guy looked a lot like that Jackie Gleason fellow we watched on TV. He was as large, laughed as loud and as much, and had the same slick, dark hair.

From the way they were acting, I could tell he was flirting with Mom and she with him. He told her those books would help us learn our subjects in school—as if he knew anything about how smart or dumb we were—and when she refused to buy, he told he'd give her some time to think it over and stop back again. After he'd visited about three or four times—usually right after lunch—Mom came out of her bedroom one day wearing a beautiful floral-print full-skirted dress. She had hose on (also known as nylons), and her hair was neatly combed and curled. She even had her lips painted rosy red. I figured she must have wanted to look extra nice for this guy named Bruce.

Then, during one of his visits, Bruce smiled down at me, which made me blush. I was not used to older people paying much attention to me, especially men, and I was always super shy around strangers. I smiled back, and he said, "Hey, sweet princess, would you like to go out to a fancy restaurant with your mom and brothers? It's lunchtime, and you must be hungry."

"That would be nice," I said. "I am hungry. Where are you taking us?"

"We're all going to The Lexington in downtown St. Paul," Bruce said. "They have great food."

So, we all climbed into his pearly-pink Cadillac. It must have been brand new because there weren't any scratches on any of the doors; it had great big wings on the back, with taillights that blinked like Rudolf's nose. Anyway, Bruce drove us to St. Paul where we ate at the nicest restaurant I had ever even seen or been in. The waiters wore fancy black suits and served our food on large gold-rimmed plates. It was my first time to taste a Shirley Temple or to eat a shrimp cocktail—and that was before the main course! I figured I was going to be really happy with Bruce visiting Mom. He loved food, and so did I—especially if it was something I had never eaten or drank before. Bruce said that there would be many more fancy lunches like this one to come. Oh boy, I was excited!

Dating, dating, dating is what Mom and Bruce did for a few months, and then, before we knew it, he had moved in with us. Life seemed fine. After maybe a couple of months, Mom and Bruce eloped. I don't know exactly where or how or when, but they came home early one Saturday evening and told us that they were married now and that Bruce was our new stepdad. I was fine with this news, but I am not so sure my brothers liked any of it, especially Mel, being that he was oldest. In fact, he was mad as hell and let everyone know it. My guess was he was missing our real dad, Nick, and didn't want to bother with a stepdad. It wasn't very long after Bruce married Mom that she told us we were moving to the scenic resort town called White Bear Lake.

I wasn't quite sure what "scenic resort" meant back then, but as we drove into town, I spotted this great big statue of a big white bear. Well, that's kind of interesting, I thought. Traffic on the main street was pretty busy, too. The sidewalks were lined with neat shops, and most of the people looked pleasant. "Well, this doesn't look too bad," I whispered to my brother Johnny. Mom then asked Bruce to drive us past the lake so we could see for ourselves just how beautiful it was. I was impressed, but I don't think Mel liked it much—or at least he didn't let on if he did.

After our brief tour, Bruce turned at the corner of Floral Drive, pulled to the side of the street, and parked his sparkling new pink Cadillac in front of a rambler-style house. We all got out of the car, stood on curb, and gazed with wonder at our new home. My blue eyes must have been bulging with excitement. The house, which was painted a dark forest green, was larger than any place we had ever lived. Better yet, the yard went on for what seemed like forever. My eyes traveled from side to side as I took in the big bushes that seemed to hold the house in from the street and form a shield from all the baseballs and footballs that I imagined we would be throwing to all of our new friends after we moved in and got settled. The grass looked lush and thick, and I could hardly wait to roll in it or climb one of those big old trees that grew along the side of the yard. (I would later learn that that hedge of dense trees grew olives, and we could harvest from our own yard for a side dish. —Here I am, thinking about food again!)

Once inside our new home, Mom said, "You kids, go check out the bedrooms and pick the one you want." This would be the first time in my life that I had my own bedroom. I couldn't believe my luck! I no longer had to share a bedroom with my brothers, who usually woke up smelly, crabby, and damp. I called first: "Mom! Mom! I want this one. *Please, please, please,* can I have the corner bedroom?" I asked. "And can we change the pink walls to a nice orange?" Mom said, "Yes, dear, that will be fine. I know how much you hate pink."

She told us we could all help pick the colors for the kitchen cabinets, countertops, and walls. This was too good to be true. What an exciting adventure! A new home, a new dad, and soon there would be new wild and crazy friends and schoolmates! Life was on a roll. I couldn't wait to move our new black-and-white speckled linoleum kitchen table with its cherry-red vinyl-covered chairs into our new kitchen. It fit perfectly and looked as bright and cheerful as I felt. Soon it would become the nesting place for all of us, the spot we would gather for many years to come—we almost always had at least two of three meals together.

On top of all this, there was a basement where we could hang a swing from the sturdy rafters and place our oversized freezer, which we needed to hold the half a cow we got from Uncle Roy,

Mom's twin brother; we only saw him now and then because his farm was way up north. There were also two large wash tubs—all we needed now was an automatic washing machine—a large game room, and another empty corner where I could set up my sewing machine and ironing board and iron. My imagination soared as I thought of all the good times we could have in this basement dancing to records, playing doctor and nurse, entertaining friends, and just having a grand old time.

I still wasn't quite sure what "scenic resort town" meant, but from what I had seen so far, White Bear Lake looked like a nice place to call home.

Getting to Know You, Getting to Know All About You

The best part about moving to White Bear was the fact that our family fit in so well with the neighborhood. Mom maybe acted a little weird sometimes, and talked with a potty mouth most of the time, and there was no denying that our family life wasn't quite like Beaver Cleaver's, but compared with the rest of the neighbors on Floral Drive, we were normal. After my brothers and I settled into our new surroundings, we learned that all the neighbor kids had cool nicknames. Our names, Melvin, Johnny, and Patty, sounded way too ordinary and boring compared with the likes of Poopy, Snuffy, Skippy, Fatty, JT, Paco, Snack Cakes, and Big Butt Boyer. Also, everyone on the street played together, fought together, and kept tabs on one another and the happenings in the 'hood. There was never any need to knock on any door; all of us kids came and went freely into each other's homes, helping ourselves to whatever food was lying about and listening to each family's latest grit and grief.

The worst neighbors, by far, were the Nicklesons. They lived around the corner and down the street, and Mom said that they set a new standard for lowlife. Their weekly episodes of drunk-and-disorderly conduct kept everyone on the block entertained and the White Bear police patrolling Floral Drive every weekend.

Then there was Slick Dick the Car Man, who looked like Bing Crosby, had a bombshell of a wife, and a different polyester suit for every day of the month—not just a week, but a *month*! He made good money selling Chevys, had a passel of kids, and lived in a neat, freshly painted house. We figured their life was nearly perfect, but that was before the bombshell exploded.

Also, every neighbor had a name: Plastic Perry Jones (because all his furniture was coated in plastic), Porky Pierre Pierce (he was as wide as he was tall at four feet nine inches) and Homely Harold Gavin (as homely as can be!), and the one everyone disliked and feared the most, Demon Darren Latooney. Unfortunately, Demon Darren was Loretta's husband, and Loretta happened to be the most vibrant, funny, and beautiful person I had ever met. She and her large brood of brats lived across the street from us, but Demon Darren never allowed Loretta to leave the house without him. That meant she had to stay inside all the time, or suffer the consequences.

My brothers called Loretta and her brood "The Loony Latooneys," and Mom regularly warned me to keep my distance when Demon Darren was around. She said he was a "control freak" (whatever that meant) and that he could be mean if he wanted to, which we all knew was true because we often heard him yelling and Loretta screaming when he came home from work. But, I loved Loretta and spent as much time with her as I possibly could. We became the best of friends, even though she was old enough to be my mom.

Yep, ours was a wacky neighborhood for sure, but thank God for that. It taught me an important lesson that's stayed with me all my life. Living on Floral Drive taught me that *quirky* and *normal* are simply two sides of the same coin—like heads and tails. Guess that's why I still enjoy meeting new people. I love trying to figure out whether they are showing me their heads or tails. Oh, I forgot to mention—my childhood nickname was The Breeze. It was either that or Patio (Patty O.). Made sense to me.

The One and Only Lovely Loony Loretta Latooney

Loretta Latooney had been a wild woman in her younger days. She told me so. She said when she was in her prime, her looks could stop a bus. All of which sounded strange to me. I wasn't exactly sure what prime meant, and I had no idea how or why a bus would stop for a particular look, prime or otherwise, but I believed her. That's because we were the best of friends.

The Latooneys lived across the street from us. Although Loretta barely stood five feet tall, everything about her was large: her family, her boobs, her soul, her spirit, her sauciness, and most of all, her wonderful singing voice. That's how I got to know her—from listening to her sing. We hadn't lived on Floral Drive very long before I heard that voice … her voice … and the happy sound of organ music coming from the house across the street every morning after the men left for work. Her children might be running around outside naked, whooping it up like wild hooligans, but Loretta sat undisturbed at her organ and sang and played in joyful bliss. Because Loretta's small-but-good-sounding organ faced our picture window, I got to watch, listen, and enjoy Loretta's performances from my front-row seat on our living-room sofa. After a few weeks of sitting by myself as the unseen audience, I couldn't stand it any longer. I knew I had to get to know this beautiful woman and share in, what I later learned she called, her happy times.

No doubt about it, Loretta was a red-haired (probably dyed), full-blooded Italian sex symbol—Mom said she was like Gina Lollobrigida—full of love and life and laughter, all of which she displayed only after her husband, the dreaded Demon Darren, had left for work. Otherwise, Loretta was a quiet mouse who never left home, never went outside, and never talked to anyone on the street unless accompanied by her hunchbacked husband, the one man everyone on the street disliked and feared. Demon Darren wasn't Italian. He was a jerk. Why or how Loretta ever hooked up with this terrible little bent-over man, I never could figure. Maybe it was because he had an important job. He worked as a social worker, so you'd think he'd have a soft heart since he was constantly helping needy people solve their problems with their families, money, and bratty kids, but it wasn't so. Instead, it seemed that he spent all his time at work trying to figure out how to keep his lovely and loving wife from enjoying life.

The good news was that Demon Darren worked Monday through Friday, from early morning to early evening. With her husband gone, Loretta could express her best side—her free-spirited side. So, she played her organ and sang her heart out. I'm sure she thanked God for that organ because it must have helped her play away the torment of her life. Speaking of God, thanks to Him, Loretta could claim another couple of hours of freedom for herself every week. Her demon husband happened to be a dedicated churchgoer who attended the First Lutheran Church religiously (no pun intended). This meant that he was gone every Sunday morning from nine until noon or maybe even one o'clock, if we were lucky. It always seemed strange to me that he didn't take lovely Loretta to church with him, especially because she sang like an angel, but she never seemed to mind staying at home. Instead, she just sat at the organ and made her own church music. I never minded that he left her behind, either. I kept watch out the living-room window, and as soon as I saw him drive away, I was off like a shot to visit Loretta.

On those precious occasions when we were alone together, Loretta would play her favorite bawdy ballads or sing songs like "My Darling Clementine" or "Sweet Georgia Brown." One time, she said, "Sing along with me, Patty. Here are the words to 'You Ain't Nothing But a Hound Dog,' by that new swivel-hipped singer, Elvis Presley. It's a really fun song to sing, and the words are easy."

"Sure," I said. "Show me how." Loretta said she'd sing the high notes and I could sing the middle and low parts since I had an alto voice. I guess that meant I had a lower song voice than hers, but I didn't care because I knew we made good sounds together. It didn't matter how good we were, or if anyone liked what they heard, we simply had a great time singing our hearts out. Every now and then, we'd hit some "sour notes" as Loretta called them, and we'd crack up laughing. Sometimes we'd laugh so hard we cried, and one time we laughed so hard, I almost peed my pants. Loretta did, and then we laughed even more. It was one of our best times together.

But I was always on the alert for Demon Darren. I kept an eye and ear open at all times for his noisy, dirty brown station wagon coming around the corner from County Road F. As soon as I saw or heard anything, I'd quietly slip out the front door and hide in the bushes until I was certain the coast was clear. Then I'd cross the street and walk home. Thank God he never saw me; otherwise, I'm sure I never would have been allowed to spend Sunday mornings with the one and only, lovely, loony Loretta Latooney.

Slick Dick, the Car Man

A Bing Crosby look-alike, who wore the flashiest polyester suits ever seen, lived down the street from us. He must have owned at least thirty of those eye-popping plaid suits. Seemed to me he had a different one for every day of the week. They reminded me of those outfits famous people wore on *The Ed Sullivan Show,* something like Dean Martin would wear whenever he was a guest singer. Anyway, this Bing Crosby look-alike was named Dick, and he happened to be the hottest Chevrolet salesman in White Bear.

Dick was a smooth talker and had hair that looked and smelled like bacon grease. It was slimy, brown, and long for his age. I had a feeling he was heavily influenced by Elvis—in a bad way, though. Still, Dick was usually polite to all the neighborhood kids, which was really all that mattered to us. However, even though he seemed like an okay kind of guy, we all called him Slick Dick, the Car Man. I often wanted to reach up and feel his slimy scalp to see if it really felt like bacon drippings, but I never did. That was probably a good thing.

In spite of his slicked-back hair, Dick's face actually was sort of handsome, for an old guy. I guess all those plaid polyester suits and his Bing Crosby looks must have been sexy to the older folks because until his fall from grace around the time he turned forty—which seemed really old back then—he sold tons of cars and trucks to nearly everyone in town. He must have made good money, too, because his house was the pride of the neighborhood, always freshly painted and nicely landscaped, and of course, he always had a shiny, new Chevrolet to drive, too. No doubt about it, if there was one man on Floral Drive to envy, it was Slick Dick.

Slick Dick was usually the top salesman at the Chevy dealership every month. He was flirty with all the adult ladies and the teenagers, too, and his bright polyester suits drew a lot of attention from strangers. All the neighbors thought he was probably fooling around on his wife, due to his flirtatious ways. We soon found out, however, that it was his Italian, dark-skinned beauty of a much younger wife who had issues with her otherwise perfect Midwest suburban life. Apparently, she was not happy. The neighborhood kids never cared much about what happened in the personal lives of the neighbors, but this time, everyone was about to get the shock of their small-town American life with some larger-than-life gossip that would spread like wildfire!

What happened was, one day, out of the blue, Dick's wife, Donna, ran off with another woman and never returned to Dick and his flashy ways. This news hit him like a ton of bricks—he had no clue that his marriage was on the rocks or that his wife now preferred to be with a woman instead of him! This happened in 1960 when such things were rare, silenced, and shunned. The locals would hush up whenever they saw Donna walking uptown in her sexy dress and high heels, hand in hand with her young babe girlfriend. Both ladies were bombshells and appeared not to care a fig about what people thought or said. They were even chatty and highly social, especially with the younger crowd. That came as a surprise to our town. It was the first time this kind of thing had been seen in uptown White Bear. Beautiful ladies holding hands and smooching! That had never happened before, I am certain.

Poor Dick never recovered from this huge shock. People had thought that he was a man of good, strong moral character built on solid Lutheran values, but the news quickly came out that he had almost immediately started drinking whiskey to escape from his out-of-control, spiraling, down-the-tubes life. Neighbors began watching and whispering whenever he pulled his new Chevrolet out of his driveway on his way to work—he could be spotted driving crazy as early as eight in the morning.

Donna also left Dick with their five kids, ages from four to sixteen, even though he was quickly losing control of his life and drinking more heavily every day. As the months wore on, he could often be seen sleeping it off (that is, being drunk) in his front yard, sometimes right in the middle of the afternoon. We all knew this because most of us kids were very active when the weather was nice, and we spent most of these days riding our bikes right past his house on our way to the lake.

After a couple of difficult years, Dick was seen wandering the streets of St. Paul, seemingly lost and completely stoned out of his mind, unable to even mumble the simplest phrase, including his own name. Soon after, his children, who now lived with their aunt and uncle in Maplewood, locked him up in the crazy ward of the Ramsey County Hospital where he has lived out the remainder of his slick, polyester life.

One time, a car salesman friend of Dick's went to visit him and gave him a ukulele. (Who knows why?) Dick quickly taught himself to play it, fairly well from what was said. (We all knew this because some nutty TV show interviewed crazy, locked-up people, and he was one of them. In fact, he appeared to be the main star!) He seemed happy and content, and began to take on the complete persona of the real Bing Crosby, even though I don't remember ever seeing Bing Crosby play a ukulele. Dick, having been called a look-alike for so long, memorized a dozen or so songs that Bing was famous for and sang them all day long while strumming his ukulele.

Dick, aka Bing, helped keep evenings in the "crazy ward" lively (so gossip had it), which drove the other crazy people happily wild, so the medication that was used to control them was no longer needed. A couple years later, the St. Paul newspaper got wind of this crazy ukulele player, and a sweet and endearing story was written up for the Sunday edition about Slick Dick and his greasy hair, his polyester suits, his wild ex-wife, and much more. It was an article worth saving.

As for Donna and her girlfriend, they lived happily ever after raising purebred standard poodles for dog shows. After they became well known as poodle breeders, they opened up a grooming saloon for *poodles only*! Eventually, they moved to Minneapolis where their type of lifestyle was more accepted and typical. The last I heard, the couple's children all ended up living highly dysfunctional but successful lives in their own private and quirky ways. And Slick Dick? He's still alive as far as I know. But if he is, he must be a hundred by now, probably still strumming his uke and singing "I'm Dreaming of a White Christmas" a la Bing.

Mom Swore like a Sailor

I would often overhear the neighbors say, "That Ruby sure does swear like a sailor when she's mad at someone," and I always wondered what that meant. Did all sailors use foul language, and if so, why? How did Mom get to know these sailors? Had she dated one in high school? We were pretty far from any ocean, and I couldn't recall ever seeing any sailors at our house, so how did she learn to talk like one? This saying just didn't make any sense to me at the time.

Meanwhile, Mom's trash-talking mouth was not only known and heard by the neighbors, but certainly by my brothers and me as well. *Jesus Christ, goddamn, shit,* and *son of a bitch* were Mom's favorite expressions. She spewed out these cuss words so frequently we actually came to think of them as terms of endearment. Johnny told me he believed his real name was Jesus Christ since Mom was usually looking at him when those words came out of her mouth. That seemed funny to me, especially because Melvin seemed more like Jesus Christ than Johnny, but maybe Johnny looked more like Jesus. Who can say? Anyway, Mom's swearing was such a daily thing that after a while I never heard it or thought much about it anymore.

Later on, as I got older, I realized that swearing is just a way of talking for some folks, one being my mom. Forget about knowing sailors; still, Mom had somehow learned to talk this way. I still hadn't figured out if this was a common, normal, natural way to speak, but I started to have an inkling that maybe, just maybe, she had learned these words from her life experiences, which hadn't always been smooth sailing. Maybe, like a sailor on rough seas, she used all these bad words because they gave her a much-needed edge or some other kind of power.

For my part, I never did learn to swear like my mother. Although I tried it now and again, it just didn't seem like a natural way to talk, so I dropped those words from my everyday vocabulary. For the most part, I only tend to use them now when the most serious things happen in my world, and I thank my mom each and every time I am pushed enough to use her sailor words. She and her cussing come through for me when necessary, and that's the good thing about bad language.

My Lovely Willow Tree

When we had lived in our neat little green home about a year, and although I loved the house, I thought our backyard was boring. It was just a big empty space. It had pretty, green grass, which was nice, but not much else. In my mind, I saw an empty canvas. I knew it needed something to bring it to life—but what?

Then one day while I was exploring the nearby woods that hemmed our neighborhood, I spied the most beautiful willow tree I had ever seen. First off, it was big for a willow—especially a willow in the middle of the woods. Somehow, even though it was surrounded by taller trees, this willow had managed to grow tall and fat. Its limbs had spread out all around, and its wispy leaves hung low to the ground, making it a perfect umbrella-shaped tree to hide and play under.

Now, even though I wasn't one to mess with Mother Nature, I couldn't resist breaking off a little branch of this most wonderful tree to take home and plant in our otherwise boring and empty backyard. I knew exactly where I would plant my lovely little twig, and I carried the branch lovingly as I continued on my walk through the woods. As I rambled about, I began noticing all the different sights and sounds of this untamed world of plants and trees. I was happy and proud to be bringing a part of it home with me, dreaming of what I believed would someday grow into the most magnificent willow tree in all of White Bear.

Mother Nature didn't seem to be too upset about my plan. In fact, I think she was pleased. A soft breeze and chirping birds seemed to signal her approval as I knelt down and dug the perfect-sized hole for my new tree. I gently set the branch in its place and covered it snugly with the dirt. Just like tucking a baby in a cradle, I thought, satisfied with my effort. Then, in all innocence, I said a prayer that my little tree would flourish like the one in the woods and become a beautiful sight for everyone passing by our yard to stop and admire.

I never had any doubts that my lovely willow tree would be impressive, and it didn't disappoint me. Every time I return to White Bear, I drive by the little green house on Floral Drive to check on my tree. It's now at least forty feet high and still growing strong. Even better, according to the neighbors, people going by still stop to admire it. It's a beauty.

Winter Picnics with the Loony Latooneys

My mom thought the Latooney neighbors were wiggy, but I happened to think they came up with the best things to do on the worst days of winter. After about the six thousandth day of sub-zero temperatures, our very nice, very Italian neighbors invited us kids to join them for a winter picnic near the St. Croix River. My brothers didn't want to go because, for some reason, they were not as fond of this family as I was, but I think the real reason was that they were being sissies, afraid of getting too cold. The frigid temperatures didn't really matter to me. I was excited to go, and I was glad to get out of the house.

When Loretta called, asking if I wanted to join them for their first-of-the-season winter picnic, I didn't hesitate for a moment. I grabbed my winter parka, wool gloves, scarf, and boots and ran across the street to their home. They had packed all the normal picnic gear and food: hot dogs, hamburgers, brats (Minnesota slang for bratwurst), and pop, which we eagerly loaded into the family station wagon along with their brood of kids. When we got to the picnic site, the sky was a deep, radiant shade of blue, and the air was somewhere between ten and twenty degrees below zero. I was not the least bit worried about freezing to death, but as it turned out, I should have been.

"What were they thinking?" Mom asked me later, when I arrived home partially frozen. Apparently, they weren't thinking because Mr. Latooney—aka Demon Darren—kept trying to get a flimsy fire going while the rest of us sat around on cement benches (the worst idea!) and waited to get our hot dogs on the fire for lunch.

From what I could gather from the looks on the other kids' faces, all of our limbs were stiffening as we pretended to enjoy this nutty idea of staying there and eating lunch while we froze to death.

To eat lunch, we would have to remove our mittens, and I wasn't about to do that. No way. I figured I'd be better off to eat my lunch with my mittens on and spill catsup all over them, rather than remove them and risk losing a finger. We were saved at last by the onset of dusk and the continually falling temperatures. Demon Darren said, "Okay, kids, let's gather up our stuff and load the car. Night's a coming on." Just as I couldn't wait to get out of the house, I now couldn't wait to go home so I could share my story with Mom and my brothers—and take a long hot bath to thaw out.

This adventure with the neighbors happened about twice each long winter, and I always looked forward to it. After all, that's what Minnesotans did for fun, or at least, that's what the loony Latooneys and I did. Mom still said we were all wiggy, but it really was fun—especially after those limbs thawed out and life continued on its merry way.

PART III
SO MUCH FOR HAPPILY EVER AFTER

Bruce Bites the Snowdrift

Shortly after we had settled into our new home in White Bear Lake, Mom and Bruce started having problems—problems of the screaming kind. Here's a bit of what I overheard one cold, gloomy day when I was supposed to be doing homework in my bedroom. Mom and Bruce were in the kitchen, and Mom was yelling at the top of her lungs while Bruce kept making excuses. "Honest, Ruby. I paid our mortgage last week. They should have gotten the check by now."

"The hell you did!" Mom yelled. "The mortgage company just called and said our payment is three weeks overdue! What did you do with that money, Bruce?"

"I swear, I sent the check in right on time," Bruce replied, sounding hurt, as if he'd been insulted because Mom didn't believe him.

"Well, while we are on the topic of money, how come there's only thirty dollars in our joint account? Where the hell did our Encyclopedia Britannica paycheck go? Huh, Bruce, huh?"

My eyes were stinging, and my ears were burning by this point. So I slithered out the front door. I'd heard enough to know that this shouting match was in no way a positive sign for our family's future togetherness. Arguments like that one, and worse, came and went every month—Mom yelling at Bruce because there was never enough money, and Bruce cowering, making excuses, and then driving off in his pink Cadillac, sometimes saying, "Honey, I'll take care of all this. Please believe me." After which, Mom would start slamming doors and crying really hard.

Mom's sobbing always got my attention, and on one particular day, I went to her and asked, "Mom, what is Bruce doing? Is he lying to you, to us? Is he not what we think? Is he a bad man?"

Mom hugged me hard and said, "That son of a bitch has to go before he drives us into the poor house! I have a strong feeling he's a fraud and a thief. Every month lately, the mortgage company has called, and the bank, too. Apparently, he's overdrawn our account more often than not. I can't take it anymore. When he comes home tonight, his bags will be out in the snow, smart books and all!"

"I'll help, Mom," I said, still hugging her with all my might. "And you can bet Melvin will help too. He doesn't like Bruce at all. Melvin's over at Ricky's house. I'll go get him right now," I said, grabbing my coat and mittens.

By the time Melvin and I returned home, Johnny was there too. Working together like the *Mission Impossible* team, the four us swiftly gathered up Bruce's stinky, cigar-smelly clothes and stuffed all his belongings into some cardboard boxes we hauled up from the basement, and dragged everything out to the front yard. We placed the boxes on a big snowdrift in clear view so he couldn't miss them, and then Melvin hung a hand-lettered sign on the top box. It said: "Bruce's Crap. Pick Up Now and Leave!"

Congratulating each other on a job well done, we trooped inside to wait and watch for Bruce to return. Well, at least Mom and the boys did. I had had enough of all this drama, so I retreated to my still newly painted orange bedroom. There, I curled up in bed and read my latest novel of everlasting love and romance. I felt bad for Mom. Bruce hadn't worked out so well after all, but at least I could hope and believe Prince Charming was somewhere out there, waiting for Mom to find him.

Mom's Mood Swings

"God damn it, you kids—leave me alone! I'm tired, I'm tired—I'm really tired!" That's what Mom would shout at us kids when she was in one of her bad moods. Then she'd slam her bedroom door and lock us out of her life for a while. When she was in one of these moods, she would stay in her room for what seemed like days.

I guess we coped okay. Bruce was gone by this time. Mom said she kicked his sorry ass out just like she'd done with Slick Nick's, but this time the reason was because "that smooth-talking son of a bitch Bruce had driven us to the poorhouse in his goddamn pink Cadillac." Anyway, my brothers and I got along during Mom's exile, cooked our own food, and managed to survive the "bad-mood times" because we always knew that she would eventually open her locked bedroom door and come out smiling, ready to resume a normal life, or as normal a life as any of us could imagine.

I often wondered what she was doing all that time locked away by herself in her bedroom and how she managed to survive her solitary confinement. I didn't worry about her though. I figured she was eating the candy that she thought she'd hidden from us kids—chocolate bars, black licorice (sometimes red, too), and other gummy caramel-like candies. Johnny and I had found her stash one day while snooping in her underwear and brassiere drawer; we knew she could stay locked in her room for maybe even a week and never die from starvation.

Another thing that puzzled me was that we never heard her leave her room to use the one and only bathroom in the house, but she must have, probably when she heard the screen door shut. I figured she must have done her thing when she knew we were out of the house and the coast was clear. Eventually, however, after each self-inflicted time-out, Mom would finally open her bedroom door and reenter our lives, acting as if nothing had happened. Once again, she'd be the loving, calm, serene, and ready-to-get-on-with-life mom I loved so much. Life went back to normal—at least until the next time.

People said that Mom suffered from mood swings, but I was never quite sure what that meant. I knew about mood rings that changed colors according to your feelings, and I loved playground swings, but I couldn't quite put the two together to make sense of mood swings. After she went to that special place for her "vacation," Mom's mood swings pretty much stopped. The newer, stronger pills she took every day evidently did their job. It wasn't until much later that I learned Mom was a hypochondriac, meaning she could act her way toward being sick if she felt like it, and she could act her way toward being well again if or when she felt like it. It was a condition. It was her condition, and our condition, throughout those early childhood years.

Learning to Fight Back

My brothers used to terrorize me. The first time, they cornered me in my room, dragged me to the bathroom, and tried damn hard to flush my foot down the toilet. The second time, they tied ropes around my ankles and wrists and hung me from the springs under my mattress. Both times, I screamed bloody murder, but no one came to my rescue. The third time they tried to get me, I was ready.

When I heard them coming toward my bedroom, I hid behind my bedroom door with a baseball bat in hand. They were trying to be sneaky, whispering and plotting outside my bedroom; but their voices were loud enough for me to overhear their plan. "Mom's at the store, so let's grab Patty and tie her up to the clothesline pole in the backyard." I held my breath and stood stick still behind the door waiting for them to open it. Melvin was the first one to come in. (I was glad because he was always the instigator of these terrorist attacks.) I blasted him with my strongest left swing, right to the back of his head. Fortunately, my swing wasn't strong enough to do him serious harm. But he went flying onto my bed, and Johnny went running in the opposite direction to hide out somewhere in the house (probably still close enough to hear what happened next).

As Melvin lay moaning, I stood over him and laughed. I said, "No more! You aren't going to pick on me anymore. I'll fight back each time you come near me and clobber you over the head with worse than you got today if you ever try again!" Stunned, he looked up at me—with a look of newfound respect. I had a feeling he was proud of my attempt to fight back. It was almost as if he was thinking, "Well, it's about time you learned to defend yourself." Now that he knew what I was capable of, I said, "Get out of here, and don't come back. Tell Johnny I'll give him the same, too, if he tries anything."

And so it went. Melvin left my room and never harassed me again. However, he eventually witnessed many future fights that I had in our front yard with the neighbor boys, whenever I felt I needed to teach them a lesson or two. Mostly, it was all in fun, but I remember one incident when I once again used force to make my point.

Here's what happened. One midsummer evening, I was washing the dishes and Johnny was drying them. Just as I was just about to scrub down the frying pan to remove the burnt crusts of the fish sticks Mom had fixed for supper, Johnny picked up a dish that I had washed and said, "This isn't clean. You missed a couple spots." I turned to him and said, "It is too clean," and because I had that frying pan in my hand and was perturbed by his criticism, I hit him over the head with it. He immediately started screaming, "Mom, she hit me!" I went running out the back door and down the street to my friend D's house to wait until this little domestic dispute blew over. Johnny had started it, but I had ended it. I later admitted that I had overreacted and told Johnny I was sorry. He also said he was sorry, really sorry. Doing dishes was a quiet event from that point on.

My brothers continued to tease and pick on me whenever they had a chance, but at least I had learned to stand my ground and fight back if I needed to do so. This was an important lesson, one that I would need to recall a few more times during my childhood. But, that's another story—or two.

Mom's Vacation

When I was nine or ten years old, my brothers and I had the good fortune to be blessed by an angel. The angel's name was Nurse Carmen, and the reason she came to us was because Mom had to go away for a little rest. Mom needed a rest from us kids because after throwing Bruce out into the street (just a year earlier), times were tough for all of us. They were especially tough for Mom since she was a single mother, and my brothers and I were evidently sometimes too much for Mom to handle.

According to Mom, Bruce was, among many other things, a money launderer. I didn't really know what that meant, but Mom tried to explain his sins and her reasons for dumping him. "Honey," she said, "he stole all our money that was in the bank. He robbed us blind." I figured that this was a good enough reason for Mom to have a nice vacation and hoped she would rest up good and return soon to be our great mom.

Meanwhile, I heard some people say that she was ready for a breakdown and, again, I didn't know what that meant. Mom was going on a little vacation, and to me, that was nothing but a good thing. Everyone needs vacations now and then, I thought. A lot my friends took family vacations every year, but our family never did. Still, it sounded like a good idea and a lot of fun.

I suppose we were all getting under Mom's skin. Johnny was eleven, Melvin was a teenager, and I was the kid sister. My brothers were mean and ornery, rough-and-tough boys, so I guessed they were the ones who had worn Mom down to a frazzled, thin, confused, and exhausted person who needed a long retreat at a special clinic in a place along the Mississippi.

Before she left on her vacation, Mom said the welfare system would be taking care of us—just until we could come up with something better or as soon as my big brother Melvin could find a part-time job. Mom hoped that we would not stay on welfare for very long because cashing in food stamps at the grocery store was embarrassing. Melvin was in high school and old enough to work; he said to Mom, "Mom, don't worry. I'll get a paper route and help with the bills." This sounded like a good plan to all of us, but Mom still needed to get away for a while and rest.

She told us where she would be staying, but I quickly forgot the name of the place when she introduced us to this really nice, sweet-faced nurse who would be caring for us during Mom's vacation. I loved this nurse at first glance. She glowed. She looked like what angels should look like, and she was here on earth, living in our house and sleeping in my mom's room for an entire month.

This was a wonderful time for me. Nurse Carmen reminded me of a TV nurse, since TV was the only place I had ever seen a nurse. She fit the role perfectly, what with her starched white nurse's dress and stiff white cap perched high on her pretty brown hair, her thick beige nurse stockings covering her shapely legs, and the dull, white-laced, thick-soled nurse's shoes that squeaked as she walked from room to room. Nurse Carmen cooked and cleaned and cared for us the entire time Mom was away. I was certain she had to be the kindest nurse in the entire world, especially when she served me bean with bacon soup, peanut butter sandwiches, and two large glasses of chocolate milk for lunch.

I'm not sure what my brothers thought of her, but I truly believed that Nurse Carmen was an angel sent from high in the clouds or maybe even from heaven. My memories of our lives with Nurse Carmen were that she was an angel of the highest order, especially when she tucked me in bed for the night and looked straight into my vibrant blue eyes (as she called them) and wished me the best dreams the world. I knew she was heaven-sent right then and there. My dreams were always cushy soft and pleasant while Carmen stayed with us.

After two short months of being away resting, Mom came home looking like a teenager with a new curly perm in her newly colored hair. She also had a handful of new prescriptions to help her deal better with the stresses of life in general and three kids in particular. I was happy to have Mom back, but I had a crying jag when Carmen left, even though she promised me she would call now and then when she could. I hoped so. I liked being cared for by an angel, and I cried hard as I watched her get into her car and drive off.

Still, it was obvious that Mom had changed during her vacation. She looked brighter, prettier, and she even wore make-up now with red lipstick, which seemed to make her smile more, just like a movie starlet. She acted calm and serene and in control, and all our lives started to improve—even our school grades went up the following school year. My brothers' fighting didn't entirely stop, but it sort of improved. What helped even more was that Mom started dating a policeman on Friday nights. There was probably more to Mom's mood swings, but we never knew for sure. We never heard any more about them, and we were happy, Mom was medicated, and all seemed right with the world.

Goodbye to Welfare

"I'm sorry, kids, I hate paying for food with food stamps," Mom said, "but we have no other choice right now."

Having just suffered through a humiliating trip to the corner grocery store, my brothers and I sat in Mom's ugly, old, dented green Studebaker like forlorn cast-offs lost on a desert island. We had only bought the basics—hamburger meat, canned peas, and white rice. There had been nothing left for any extras, like chips or cola or even a candy bar. It was the middle of the month, and when it came time to pay, the cashier had made some snide remark about hoping we could make do as she counted out what was left from our monthly allotment of food stamps. We hoped so too, but we didn't like to be reminded of the fact. It was embarrassing and even a little intimidating, but Johnny and I didn't know enough to be afraid of what might happen if we couldn't make do.

Only Melvin seemed to grasp the gravity of the situation. His face and eyes looked as dark and cloudy as the wintry Minnesota sky hovering above us. "Mom, I'm going to get a job and get us off welfare," he said with the finality of total determination. "I'll look for a job first thing in the morning."

Mel was already in high school, old enough to work, and by the end of the week, he had kept his promise. He had a job selling newspapers. He was proud and ambitious and dauntless—waking up each morning by five, heading out on his route like a mailman, in rain or sleet or snow, and even on those rare days of welcoming sunshine, delivering his papers to neighbors far and near. Everyone counted on him for their daily news, and he never let them down.

Not only was Melvin the most efficient paper boy in White Bear, he was also the most proficient at making his collections. If a customer wasn't available or didn't have the money on collection day, he would keep going back and wait patiently and politely in the kitchen or on the porch until every customer had written out a check for the amount due. He was persistent to say the least, and he never forgot who did or did not pay regularly and/or tip adequately. From his very first paycheck, Mel saved every nickel (at least that's what Mom said), and it wasn't too long before he had earned enough to get us off welfare for good. Handing over the $300 he had saved from his paper route, he told Mom, "I never want to use welfare and food stamps ever again." Mom said, "Great! I can't wait to call those bastards and tell them we don't need their damn handouts anymore." (I really thought he had learned from Bruce how to patiently collect from each and every customer.)

After that, we never again took money from the government or anyone else. With Mel helping out, Mom had money in her checking account and paid for our groceries, and anything else she wanted, with a huge smile on her face and a whole lot of pride in her heart for her hard-working son. Before long, Mel also had his own savings account, but he always set aside a few extra dollars for our weekly trip to the Dairy Queen where he treated us to whatever we wanted. Mom and I loved their Dilly Bars, and we looked forward to sitting on the picnic benches in front of the DQ stand and enjoying the sweet taste of a treasured midsummer treat. Thanks to Melvin, life was good, and we were free from debt again.

Two for One

Mom was always frugal. She had to be because times were tough and money was short when we were kids, something for which she blamed Bruce. But I think Mom was born a bargain hound. I just never knew how much she loved to bargain until I split my head open one day while sledding.

It's a good thing I had my big brother to save me from freezing to death in a pool of blood the day we decided to go sledding. It was the day after the Twin Cities had four feet of fresh snow dumped on, right before Christmas. Melvin is the hero of this story. He came to my rescue this cold, snowy day—and a couple times thereafter that I recall. Anyway, he did what big brothers do, and he did it well because he was older and bigger and had developed more muscles than either Johnny or I had. He saved me, his one and only (at that time) little sister, from a bloody death in frigid weather on the icy White Bear Lake. The year was 1963, the first winter in our new town.

After the record snowfall, Mel, Johnny, and I trudged out to the thickly frozen lake for an exhilarating day of fun. I was wearing my new blue snowsuit, which covered most of my body but left my face and forehead bare. In 1963 (and probably before then), sleds were made of wood and metal. The pointy metal part of a front runner rammed right into my forehead as a neighbor kid came zooming down the small hill smack dab in front of me. The front of his sled slammed into my uncovered forehead, causing a large crack to open and blood to spew out. I had no chance to move out of his way because I was lying on my tummy and preparing for my big push off. My fun for that day ended right then.

All the kids rushed over to help me, and one of the smarter kids yelled for my big brother who, they told me later, was flirting with a girl near the frozen solid dock. Meanwhile, blood was shooting out of my forehead turning my very blonde hair a dark maroon color. I was quickly becoming drenched in blood and started losing consciousness—at least as much consciousness as a little bit of a girl can lose—as it ran down my body and arms and covered my new snowsuit with a deep-red sticky goo. Melvin raced across the ice to save me. He gently picked me up in his newly developing strong arms and carefully carried me home.

Mom was frantic when she saw me, but she took immediate action. She rushed me off to the emergency room where they proceeded to put fifteen stitches in my swollen, round head. I was in a semi-coma, or at least a form of shock, since I had lost a gazillion gallons of blood. It was scary! All I really remember is that I was staring at a very white ceiling when someone gave me a shot that knocked me out for the ten count.

I still have a scar where all those tiny, black, very strong stitches sewed up my forehead, but what I couldn't see and didn't know about until later were the stitches on the top of my head. While I was still passed out, Mom told the doctors to remove a bump on the top of my head. Apparently, I was born with this strange little bump that was right in the center of the top of my head. The bump often opened up and bled when Mom brushed my hair too hard, so while I was passed out anyway and getting one part of my head stitched up, Mom asked the doctors if they could go ahead and remove that darn bump while they were at it.

What a deal! Two for one!

I recovered from this accident quickly and only missed one week of school—the week of our semester math tests—Hooray! By the following week, I was so ready to go back to school because I had a great story to share with all my classmates, many of whom were also on the lake the day of my fateful blood bath. I figured they were probably wondering if I had survived since the last time they had seen me I looked like a bloody zombie in my brother's arms. However, once I went back to school, I had to explain why I didn't want to take off my ski cap. I couldn't tell everyone that the top of my head had been shaved so the doctors could remove that darn bump, so I told them that I liked my new hat so much I wanted to keep it on all day while at school. Thank goodness, the teachers and students believed me because I sure didn't want to tell them Mom worked a deal with the doctors.

Good ole' Mom never lost her bargaining sense—not even during an emergency.

Mom's Saturday Night Dance

If it hadn't been for that Lawrence Welk guy and Mom, I probably would never have learned to dance the polka, or for that matter, anything else. Mom loved to dance. She said it made her feel young and happy, so she looked forward to her weekly dates with Lawrence. It didn't matter that he was miles away in some Hollywood TV studio; Mom never let anyone or anything interfere with their Saturday night dance.

Mel and Johnny would disappear as soon as they heard the first bubbly notes of what Mom and Lawrence called his "Champagne Music." Mom never seemed to mind my brothers' absence, but she always called out to me as soon as those sugary-sweet smiling people on the screen started singing and dancing. Music got Mom off the couch. Whether she heard a familiar tune or not, Lawrence's Saturday night programs gave her a chance to "shake her stuff" and teach me a thing or two.

"Patty, get in here," she would say, "so I can teach you how to polka" (or cha-cha, or waltz, or whatever the dance craze of the day was). I was probably ten when all this started, and I dreaded every minute of it. I often replied, "Oh, Mom, I don't feel like dancing tonight," but Mom wasn't one to take no for an answer. She would come into my bedroom, take me by the hand, drag me to the living room, and tell me, "Oh, honey, this will be fun." We all wanted Mom to be happy, so to keep the peace, I went along. But our dancing was more funny than fun. However, as Mom led and I followed, I eventually learned to dance the polka and the waltz, a bit of two-step swing, and whatever other one-two-three-four dance step Bobby Somebody and his current dance partner were promoting that week.

Mom always said Lawrence was "one of us," a neighbor, and we should support him. I never understood what she was talking about. I later learned that Lawrence was an accordion player from one of the Dakotas—North? South? ... Not much difference between the two. Besides, it didn't matter to me. What did matter was the fact that even though I had resisted Mom's persistence, I had learned to dance. Even as the hard rock music of the '70s wiped out the soft syrupy sounds of that Lawrence guy and his look-alike robots, I was confident knowing that I could "shake my stuff" as good as or better than the best—Mom.

Years later, when I was called upon to attend the weddings and funerals of my Polish relatives, I realized what a gift my mother had given me. Every special occasion, be it a baptism, confirmation, marriage, or funeral service, is celebrated with song and dance and food.

St. Augustine is credited with saying, "You must learn to dance; otherwise the angels will not know what to do with you." Funny thing, I can still hear my mother's voice echoing something similar to that as she called, "Get in here so I can teach you the polka. You'll need to know how to dance it someday."

PART IV
MY AGE OF INNOCENCE

Lovely Loretta: Free at Last

Loretta Latooney was not only a great singer and organ player she also made the most delicious spaghetti ever. Compared with Mom's bland and tasteless sauce, Loretta's was thick and rich, chock-full of hot peppers and flavored with lots of exotic and unfamiliar spices that Mom evidently either didn't like or had never heard of. When Loretta was cooking spaghetti, mouth-watering aromas would float out her kitchen window and drift across the street to our backyard. All it took was one whiff for my taste buds to go wild.

"Mom, Loretta's cooking spaghetti. Can I eat dinner over there?" I'd ask with eager anticipation. Mom always said yes because she knew I had a taste for spicy foods, but she also never let me go without issuing her standard warning. "Just be careful, Patty. Darren is a control freak. He can be mean if he wants to be, so watch yourself when you're around him."

"Yes, Mom, I will," I promised, and I always kept that promise.

No doubt, there was something creepy about the guy, but it wasn't enough to keep me away from one of Loretta's spaghetti suppers. Thank God Loretta loved me because I got to be a regular, expected visitor on Spaghetti Nights. Each time I'd knock on their back door, just as they were all sitting down to eat, she'd greet me with, "Come on in, Patty. I saved you a seat next to me." I always felt as if I was being treated like a special guest, but sometimes, I wondered if this bothered the rest of the Latooneys. No ever seemed to mind my being there. I was just another kid at the table, until one evening when Demon Darren appeared to be in a particularly foul mood.

On this particular night, I could sense that something wasn't quite right with everyone. But the smell and taste of Loretta's spaghetti was so tempting, I figured no one, not even Demon Darren, could ruin my appetite. Then I caught him staring at me, funny like. His steely brown eyes seemed to be burning a hole in my forehead. Finally, he looked me straight in the eye and said, "How's your mother doing, Patty? Is she dating yet?"

I was shocked to hear him ask this because it didn't seem like a topic for dinner conversation to me. With Mom's warning to be careful echoing through my head, I answered, as politely as possible, "I don't think so, but she's doing real good, thank you. She just had a permanent yesterday, and her hair is beautiful." I added this detail as proof of her well-being.

To this, Darren replied, "Well, I hope she finds a good man one of these days. Every woman needs a man." At this point, all the kids were staring at me, waiting to see what I'd say next. I could feel my cheeks start to flush, and I was biting my tongue hard to keep from saying what I was thinking, which was ... he needed to shut up and mind his own business. He's not a good man. He's a bad man. What does he know anyway? Not much, that's for sure.

Mom had already been through enough with Bruce. Here I was talking about her beauty, and all Demon Darren cared about was her finding a man. What a sick-o! I thought, returning his stare with as blank a look as I could manage. I wasn't about to tell him about her new boyfriend, Howie. No way. Especially since Howie was a policeman and could easily arrest him for how he mistreated Loretta all the time.

After this conversation, I sort of lost my appetite for Loretta's spaghetti, that is, unless I was absolutely certain Demon Darren was working late and wouldn't be home for supper. But, at least this story has a happy ending. A short while later, Mom did marry her new boyfriend, Howie, and he was indeed a good man—not at all like Nick or Bruce, or that creep, Darren, who, in fact, the police eventually arrested for beating up on Loretta. As for Loretta, after many bad years living with Mr. Hunchback, she was freed when the jerk finally died. He had had serious health issues, supposedly because he was a chain smoker and drank too much beer, but I always believed he was just rotten to the core and that's what killed him.

With Demon Darren out of her life for good, Loretta was free at last. One of first things she did was get on a city bus and ride into St. Paul all by herself. There, she walked the charming streets of downtown, ate and drank in the local diners and restaurants, and managed to pick up a few admirers along the way. Later on, she colored her flowing, wavy hair a gorgeous flaming red, and she even started to drink a bit of booze, mostly beer. I was happy to see my favorite and most eccentric best lady friend begin to open up to the world like a budding flower. However, Loretta's blossoming didn't stop with trips to St. Paul. She eventually took all the money her cheapskate husband had saved up in his personal accounts and began traveling to foreign lands with a new and different "companion" every time. Her kids were off at school by now and apparently didn't mind—and maybe even supported—their mom's new lifestyle.

Although Loretta really seemed to enjoy being on her own, she would occasionally bring one of her "young bucks" (that's what she called them) home. Even at my young age, I was struck by how handsome these guys were and how willing they were to do anything for Loretta. I so admired her for her gusto and extravagant behavior. My young face beamed with delight whenever she bragged about her conquests. I didn't think she was a bad woman at all. That's because she wasn't. She was simply giving me pointers on dating, which I desperately needed, since I was about to start doing that any time now.

As years passed, Loretta continued to live it up royally. She even recorded an album of her best organ playing and singing. It wasn't a smash hit, but it did make it all the way to the Minneapolis markets. The White Bear Lutheran Church didn't like it one bit, but who cared? Her kids were happy that their mom was happy, and I was happy to just hang out and sing along with Loretta whenever she was in town, which wasn't very often anymore.

Looking back, I realize now what a true inspiration Loretta was for me. From her, I learned that life can change, life can improve, and life can be a huge adventure. However, the most important lessons I learned from being a part of Loretta's life are: 1) all things are possible for those who wait, and 2) boyfriends can be a lot more fun than husbands. I remembered those lessons later in life when faced with some tough personal decisions.

How Mom Met Howie

Too bad Bruce didn't turn out so well as a husband or father. I was ten or so when Mom tossed him and his fancy clothes and strong cologne into the street. The problems started happening about six months after Mom came back from her rest; she had been very calm and happy up until this time. Not long after her return home, Bruce started to haunt Mom by driving by our house, shining a super bright spotlight into her bedroom window, and waking her up and scaring her.

Mom said that Bruce was driving another pink, new-model Cadillac (where he got the money, we never knew). He had some sort of spotlight attached to his new car, either by the outside mirror or on top of the car, and he drove by nightly shining it in Mom's bedroom—right when he thought she would be sleeping. I was sleeping, so I never heard or saw any of this, but I would hear all about it the following morning.

After one too many times of this happening, Mom asked Melvin to call the police in the hopes that we could catch Bruce in the act. Mom was scared out of her wits—that's what my brothers told me. Melvin said, "Sure, Mom, I'll call right now. Bruce has gone nuts, and we need to catch him! He must be insane!"

A nice policeman came by the next night around eleven, and Mom anxiously explained what had been happening for the last few weeks. The nice policeman sat with her, calmed her down, and stayed for as long as needed. This nice policeman's name was Howie, and he came by for a few nights in a row. He would park an unmarked police car a block away and come to stay with us. He did this until the one night when the police were able to surround Bruce in his nice new, sterling-pink Cadillac and take him to the slammer. I was not awake to witness this, but I always felt that even though Bruce appeared to be a nice person to me, he really was not a nice person at all. He stayed in the county jail for a while. Everything calmed down, and Mom started going out on Friday nights to go to dinner and dancing on Howie's night off work.

I think it was love at first scare—and a romance began. Mom put on red lipstick, that new Avon color for the season, and bought a new flowered dress. The two started going on dates, which sometimes included dancing, movies, and fancy dinners. Our home was beaming with a feeling of joy.

What seemed like six months later, Mom and Howie called a family meeting. Little did we three kids know that a bit of hanky-panky had been going on. Mom and Howie sat us down after six months of constantly being together, and Mom said, "Kids, Howie and I are going to have a baby and are to be married as soon as arrangements can be made with the church." Together, we three shouted, "What? Really? When?" It was all happening too fast for my little mind to absorb, but I was very excited.

The only one who didn't appear excited was Melvin. He didn't seem thrilled at all, and I didn't realize until much later how he really felt that exciting day. He was pissed because he still thought Mom and Nick, our real dad, would get back together. How wrong he was for thinking that—it would never happen.

A while after this wonderful news, Johnny and I raced outside, hopped onto our bikes, and rode up and down McKnight Road shouting from the top of our lungs, "Mom's having a baby! Mom's getting married! A baby! A new dad! Wow! Wow! Wow! Did you hear us? Mom's having a baby!"

We were thrilled for Mom—this was the beginning of a fine romance and a secure father figure in our lives and in our home, finally. I prayed that this love affair would last.

My Perfect Dress for Mom's Wedding

On most Saturday nights, Mom turned on the TV at eight o'clock to watch *The Lawrence Welk Show*. I often joined her, even though she made me dance with her during some of the songs. This seemed corny to me, but it was fun at the same time. Mom really loved this show, and she especially enjoyed the McGuire Sisters, who were often Mr. Welk's special guests. I thought they were special, too, because they really were sisters and they were beautiful. But, what impressed me the most was the fact that their dresses always matched.

One night, about three months before Mom and Howie got married, we tuned into the Welk show, and there were those sisters again. This time, they were wearing the most delicate, frilly dresses I had ever seen. The sisters looked as sweet as they sang, like angels floating in a cloud of light pink chiffon. I said, "I love that dress, Mom. Isn't it the most beautiful dress you've ever seen?"

"Yes, honey, it is a beautiful dress," Mom said, but her voice sounded as though she had something else on her mind.

Little did I know then that Mom had been searching for a special outfit for me to wear at her upcoming wedding. I was to be her flower girl, and she wanted to find me the perfect dress for this happy occasion. Much to my surprise, about a week before the wedding, Mom came home one afternoon and said, "Come here, Patty, I want you to try on your flower girl dress." When I walked into the bedroom, I couldn't believe my eyes. There on the bed lay a delicate, frilly cloud of light-pink chiffon. Somehow, Mom had figured out a way to get me the exact same dress we had seen on TV.

We were so busy at the time with all the wedding plans that I never had a chance to ask her how she managed to get that absolutely beautiful, perfect dress for me. My imagination told me that she had called Lawrence Welk himself and had ordered it special made by the same dressmaker who made all those matching dresses for the McGuire Sisters. Years later, I finally figured out that the only way she could have possibly come up with my perfect dress was to have Grandma make it.

Maybe Grandma had seen the same show, or maybe Mom had described the dress to her. Either way, I'm guessing it was Grandma who created my beautiful dress. She was an expert seamstress who was good at copying designs and working with all kinds of fabrics. Since she already had my measurements from my last visit when she had given me one of her sewing lessons, I suppose she was able to piece together a pattern and fashion that perfect dress for me to wear at Mom's wedding.

The following week, I proudly strutted down the aisle ahead of Mom wearing my pale pink, fluffy chiffon dress with matching shoes and gloves and hat (also made by Grandma). I felt so special that day—like a TV or movie star—and just as beautiful as one of those McGuire sisters on Mr. Welk's Saturday night show.

My Baby Sis, Kris

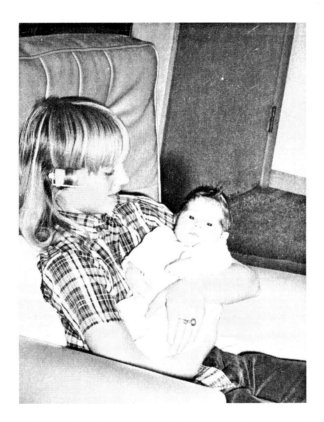

It wasn't too long after Mom married Howie that he took her to the hospital so she could have her baby. When she returned home, Mom walked through the front door carrying a little bundle wrapped up tightly in a couple of cuddly blankets. If there was a baby in there somewhere, I certainly couldn't see it. The only thing sticking up out of the cloud of pink flannel was a thick patch of black hair. For all I knew, it could have been a puppy, or maybe even a kitten, curled up in Mom's arms. Mom looked pale but happy. She told me sit down on the couch and then gingerly placed the tiny bundle in my lap. "Say hello to you new sister, Patty," she said. "Her name is Kris, with a K." That sounded okay to me. K-R-I-S. How else would you spell it? I wondered.

"Look, at all that silky, raven-black hair," she said. "Where that came from, I'll never know." It was a mystery to me, too, since Mom was blonde and Howie was as bald as a cue ball. "Hold her gently, Patty. She has a frail heart," Mom said, her voice quivering with a strange mixture of fear and courage.

I was twelve at the time, full of wonder at the sight of this new life yawning and stretching in my arms. "What do you mean *frail*?" I asked. "Is her heart okay? Will she grow up like the rest of us?"

Mom took a deep breath and almost whispered her reply. "Yes, she will grow up strong and healthy just like you and your brothers. Don't worry. Just look at her. Isn't she as sweet as can be?"

Dropping the subject of her frail heart, I looked down at my baby sister cradled snugly in my supportive arms. She must have sensed my attention because she opened her eyes and looked up at me with a curious expression. In an instant, it seemed as if we had known each other forever. Gazing into her eyes, I began to wonder what it would be like to have a sister to share the bullying burden of a pair of big brothers. I'd have to teach her to be on guard once she got to walking—no, once she got to be crawling, since they weren't about to wait that long to start tormenting her.

This little sis really was as cute as a button. She was born with her very own unique facial characteristics, which meant she didn't look a lick like any of the rest of us. Besides having a full head of dark hair, her face was long and oval-shaped, not at all like my round, blonde-haired head or Melvin's square-jawed face. Mom said that was because Kris was half Danish (Howie's side) and half Polish with a twist of English (our side.) I figured that was as good an explanation as any. Besides, it mattered neither way. She belonged to us, and we belonged to her, for better or worse.

All in all, Kris was a good baby, which meant she didn't cry all night as I'd been warned by my friends who had already suffered through the new baby routine. However, she did develop a number of food allergies and ended up to be a finicky eater; but that was okay too. All the more for the rest of us. Kris's heart condition wasn't mentioned again, at least not for the next eight or ten years. Mom had assured everyone that the baby's frail heart would be fixed once it grew large enough and strong enough to close the hole at its center.

I didn't understand any of this at the time I was holding this little black-haired bundle, but Mom explained, "Your little sister was born with a hole in her heart, so you'll have to be gentle with her. She may not have your strength or stamina, Patty, so play nice."

I couldn't imagine anyone with a hole in the heart, let alone an itty-bitty baby, surviving the harsh realities of a Minnesota winter, so I did my best to take care of my little sister. My brothers either didn't listen to the warnings and predictions or didn't care about this little bundle with the breakable donut heart because as she grew bigger and stronger, she was just like me, fair game for all their pranks and hijinks. Maybe that helped toughen her up some. All in all, even though she occasionally got tossed about and teased by Melvin or Johnny, baby Kris survived, and we all celebrated when, as a teenager, she finally got her heart fixed for good.

After putting up with two pesky brothers all my life, having a cute little sister to play with was sort of fun. One of our favorite pastimes was playing "beauty parlor." She loved to have me French-braid her long, black, silky hair, and in exchange, I let her roll my even longer, thicker, blonde hair up in sponge curlers, and then comb it out and tie twisting ribbons and knotting bows to my curls just to make me look silly. Since I loved to act silly anyway, I didn't mind it at all. It was the special bonding experience that matter most, and besides, no harm done. Our hair survived the abuse.

Supper at Six

Once Mom married Howie and my baby sis Kris arrived on the scene, our lives settled down into a real Ozzie-and-Harriet routine. Well, almost. Since Howie was a police officer working the afternoon shift, the police scanner, positioned in a place of honor in our living room, was always on when he was duty. It screeched and squawked like a mutant parrot, but Mom monitored all the calls and kept an ear out for any hint of danger or cause for concern. Most of the time, things were pretty quiet in and around White Bear unless, of course, the Nicklesons were drinking again or Demon Darren was beating up on Loretta. That being the norm, most nights, Howie made it home for supper, which was always served promptly at six. Being on time was a top priority for us kids because Mom served her meals with split-second precision. As soon as Howie's patrol car pulled into the driveway, we took our seats and served our plates. No time to waste while Howie was on his supper break.

Now that Howie was on the scene, meal times were good times at our house. Mom was a great cook—one of the best in the neighborhood (if you didn't count her attempts to cook Italian or any other spicy dishes). Whatever she cooked, she made from scratch, and it was always tasty and filling. I usually made the desserts, mostly brownies, cakes, or cookies, and Johnny baked the pies. I hated rolling dough since it stuck to everything, but he didn't seem to mind so much. During the supper hour, we all sat around the kitchen table and shared the experiences of our day, like the fights I got into with the neighbor boys, the rocks and shells Kris found by the lake, or Johnny's adventures in the woods finding a sick bird or making a new friend. After supper, while Johnny and I cleaned the kitchen and washed the dishes, Kris and Howie would move to the living room where they would play cards until he had to leave again.

When I was a little girl, I loved my Barbie dolls and dresses with flowing ruffles. Kris grew up loving rocks and shells, sticks and stones, and anything involving numbers. Numbers were our major difference. I was never very good with numbers and struggled through every math class until I finally passed all the required courses to graduate from White Bear High. Kris, however, aced all of her math classes, probably because she learned all her numbers early on playing cards with Howie.

Nightly card games were a ritual in our house. As soon as supper was over and everyone was excused, Howie and Kris would settle themselves in the living room. Howie, with his attention split between the police scanner and his precious daughter, would shuffle, deal, and then explain the rules of innumerable card games. Playing cribbage was Kris's favorite game of all, yet they also played gin and any other game that took just two players. Just the two of them. That was the unspoken rule. It was okay, though. The rest of us understood. This was their special bonding time. When the hour was up, Howie would go back to his beat, and Kris would get her bath and go to bed, with numbers still swirling through her head.

Guess that was the biggest difference between Kris and me. I was athletic—a tomboy when necessary, capable of taking on any of the neighborhood boys if I had to, which I did at least once a week in my preteen years. Kris was more like Johnny. She didn't care much for running sports, even though her legs were lean and strong and inches longer than mine. Instead, she preferred moving at a slower pace and didn't seem to mind, in fact was even proud of, the fact that she aced all her math courses while I had to struggle with all numerical concepts. I was good at running, jumping, and fighting back, and Kris was good at adding, subtracting, multiplying, and dividing. Eventually, we agreed to call our differences even.

Ladybugs, Brothers, & Badass Bees

Ladybugs are cute, and they're good for a garden. Some people even consider them a good luck omen. One day, one of those good-luck bugs crawled into my ear, my left ear it was, and never came out—or so the story goes.

I don't remember much about it, but from what my brothers told me, Mom and I were outside trimming some shrubs around the house when a ladybug landed on my shoulder.

"Oh, look Patty," Mom said, "a ladybug likes you. That means you're going to have good luck." But, just as I turned my head to look at my shoulder, the ladybug fluttered her wings, flew into my ear, and disappeared.

"Honey, I saw it go in, but it hasn't come out. Shake your head from side to side so the little guy can fall out." Well, I shook and shook back and forth and bobbled my head around and around. Mom and my brothers watched and waited, but from what I was told, the ladybug never did come out. I don't know where it ended up or whether having a ladybug inside my head brought me any good luck, but my brothers always insisted it made its home in my brain and eventually died there, dried up, and fell out flake by flake. I wasn't sure if they were telling me the truth or just being flaky. Probably the latter.

*****

Minnesota has bugs, lots of bugs—and bees, honeybees, hornets, wasps, yellow jackets, and probably a few more. Then there are the water bugs, gnats, and flies—small flies, house flies, horse flies, dragon flies—and, of course, the ubiquitous mosquitoes. Minnesota mosquitoes are brutal! They look and sound like World

War II B-52 bombers, and they can suck blood whenever and wherever, even through a heavy wool sweater or a pair of thick jeans. During the summer, these bugs and bees are everywhere, and all of them are capable of biting and making the skin swell up, causing hives, or worse yet, even death. I know this to be a fact because it almost happened to me.

One warm summer day, while I was riding my bike around the lake, a hornet flew into me head on and stung me on my right arm. At the time, I thought nothing of it and continued to pedal my bike toward home. I still had about five or six miles to go when I noticed I was feeling dizzy. I looked down and saw my arm turning bright red and swelling up to double its size. Next, I started to have trouble breathing, and I had to fight to keep from passing out and swerving my bike off the road into traffic or the drainage ditch. I really wanted to crash and call it quits, but I knew I had to keep going.

Somehow, I made it home, dropped my bike, and collapsed on the front lawn. "Mom, Mom!" I called. "Help! I'm stung! I'm stung! Call Howie!" Mom heard my cries and, after coming outside and witnessing the horror of my condition, ran back inside and called Howie at work. The police arrived within minutes. They rushed me to the hospital, where I was immediately injected with a drug to stop my allergic reaction from ending my life and ruining this otherwise pleasant summer day.

According to my brother, Johnny, I woke up later with a stunned look on my face. He said I looked as if I had just seen a ghost, which sounded funny to me. I hadn't seen a ghost, but I had felt a speedy rush in my veins and had seen some Technicolor visions flashing through my mind. Everyone said I was lucky I had survived, and I wondered if maybe that ladybug was still hanging out somewhere in my body. Anyway, after I recovered from the bee-sting shock, the hospital doctor sent me home, but not before giving Mom instructions on how to give me an immediate injection, along with some seriously strong bee-sting pills just in case it ever happened again. My brothers called it "Patty's Recovery from Death Kit." Good thing mom had that kit, because I ended up needing it.

That fall, Howie took us all to the Minnesota State Fair (which just so happens to be the best state fair in the world!). We were having a great day, enjoying the sights and all the good food. In fact, it happened while we were sitting at picnic table eating brats and mini donuts and drinking pop. Another stupid hornet landed on my hand, this time between my thumb and first finger, and before I could shoo it away, it stung me like nobody's business right in front of everyone—Mom, Howie, Johnnie, and lots of other people sitting close by. Mom grabbed her purse and handed Howie the syringe. He jabbed the needle deep into my hand to keep me from passing out—or worse, far worse. I went from a whimpering kid fading away into la-la land to zinging awake like a Superwoman ready to save the day, thanks to the adrenalin boost I got from the treasured liquid in that vial of life.

It had been another close call. I remember thinking that maybe I really did have a lady bug in my brain. However, not being one to take foolish chances or tempt fate, I continue to keep my "Recovery from Death Kit" with me to this day, and regardless of my Ladybug Luck, I still say, "Thank you, Jesus," when I remember my close encounters with those badass bees.

Summertime Fun

Growing up on Floral Drive meant spending your entire summer outside—day and night—and being outside after dark meant pulling pranks on the neighbors. Most of the neighborhood kids were rambunctious, including Johnny, me, and few other amateur hoodlums, but our pranks were usually innocent. Although a few of our hijinks might have been a little borderline, we always managed to keep things just this side of the law. Besides, since we never got caught in the act, no one could ever pin anything on us. I guess it was just pure luck that we always managed to get away just in time, or maybe it was because we could all run really fast.

On one particularly warm and boring Friday night, Dougy, Poopy, Fatty, JT, Johnny, and I decided to move the Anderson's backyard swing set onto their front lawn. Mrs. Anderson always kept her curtains closed after dark, so it was easy to sneak around the house without being seen, but it was a lot harder not to be heard, what with the creaking metal frame and our stifled giggles. After a little time and effort, we finally maneuvered it to a spot right in front of their picture window, so when they opened their drapes in the morning, the swing set would be in plain view. We figured that maybe they'd haul it away after that, since nobody played on it anymore anyway.

With that prank successfully completed, we moved on to Mrs. "Pigmy Lady" Pierce. Mrs. Pierce measured just barely four feet five inches if she wore high heels and stood up tall, but what she lacked in size, she made up for with attitude. We all agreed she was way too short and sassy for her own good and could use some gentle harassment. Seeing the TV light flickering in her living room, we guessed Mrs. Pierce was propped in her easy chair, probably nodding off with a cold Pabst in her hand. The night was still young, so we rang her doorbell a couple of times and then ran across the street and hid behind the lilac bushes that blocked the view from her front porch. Opening the door with a yank, she yelled, "Where are you brats? Do that again, and I'll call the cops. You hear? I'm gonna catch you next time, you little shits!" Laughing our heads off beneath the lilac branches, we waited for her to slam the front door and turn out her porch light before proceeding to our next activity.

Since we had had so much fun moving the Anderson's swing set, we decided to try moving the Allen's rusted, lime green, Volkswagen bug from their driveway to their backyard. That prank was actually easier than moving the swing set. No one on Floral Drive ever bothered to lock their car doors, especially if they owned a rattletrap VW. We figured most likely, the Allen's were hoping someone would steal the old heap, but who'd want it? Poopy, the only one of us who knew how to drive a standard shift, squeezed in behind the wheel and put the car in neutral. Then the rest of us pushed while he steered. It seemed like it took forever because the old car didn't roll very well on the soft, wet grass, but at least it was quieter than the creaky swing set. We finally parked the ugly bug right at the edge of the Allen's beautiful, newly built—and only one on the block—swimming pool. Oh, how we wished that we could have been flies on Mrs. Allen's kitchen wall the next morning when she looked out and saw her dirty old car parked by the side of her sparkling clean pool. Maybe she'd think she was losing her marbles and had parked it there herself, or maybe—just maybe—she'd know who the kids were that had put it there. Again, we were lucky and never got caught.

Moving cars and swing sets and running from ringing doorbells were just some of our mischievous summer evening teenage pranks. We also had fun stealing from various vegetable gardens, and one time, we even took some of Old Man "Jumbo" Jones' prized roses, wrapped them in a newspaper, and placed a nice, yet funky, bouquet on the doorstep of "Homely Harold" Galvin, along with a note that said, "I have always loved you. Please come and visit me soon. Love, Jumbo Jones." Homely Harold was the one boy on Floral Drive who never seemed to go outside and who never had a girlfriend in his entire life. Shucks, he hardly had any friends at all. As for Old Man Jones, he was a puffy-faced, super-sized, sugary-sweet Pillsbury dough man who loved to flirt with all us girls when we walked by his house. We all agreed that he deserved this prank.

We learned a few days later from Dougy, who lived next door to Jumbo and had the bathroom window open, the one that faced his driveway, that Homely Harold had gone over to Old Man Jones's place while he was in the side yard watering his forever not-so-green grass. Dougy reported that Harold had been more than just a little pissed and had greeted Jumbo with something like, "Hey dumbass, what makes you think I would want anything to do with you? Stop leaving me your stinking roses and love notes. I'm not the least bit interested in you, you stupid old man!"

This outburst evidently took Old Man Jones by surprise, but then, after realizing that it must have been one of our pranks, he told Harold, "It wasn't me, dear boy. I never wrote you any note, and I sure as hell didn't give you any of my prize-winning roses. I bet it was Dougy and his damn friends who pulled this trick." To that, Homely Harold said, "Those shits! When I catch them at this, I'm going to tell my dad, and he'll take care of them, once and for all!" The only problem with Harold's reasoning was that he never caught us at our pranks. Thank you, Jesus!

In fact, the only one who ever got caught was my brother Melvin. This happened when he and his buddy LP (otherwise known as Lard Pail) Lund, "borrowed" Mr. Lund's brand-new pickup and helped themselves to a pile of lumber from the Baumgartner's garage. Mr. Baumgartner was a local builder and owned the largest garage in the neighborhood. LP and Skip loaded up enough of Mr. Baumgartner's lumber to build their own garage and then hauled it away to a warehouse in St. Paul. They slipped up when the warehouse manager saw what they were unloading from the bright red truck that still had the dealer plates on the back. Realizing full well that neither boy was Mr. Lund, he promptly called the St. Paul police department who, in turn, called the White Bear Police department, who then came and hauled both boys off to spend a long night in the local jailhouse. Melvin and LP ended up as busted as their prank, but this prank was way, way too much. It was over the top—nothing innocent or mischievous about it. They had been up to no good and deserved their long, drawn-out evening in the White Bear jail.

Mom and Howie were embarrassed, to say the least, by Melvin's misdeeds, and within six months, Melvin had moved out. Maybe he was embarrassed by what he got caught doing, too. So shortly after that, Melvin got his own apartment, not one with Skip, who Howie said had been a bad influence on him. According to Howie, Skip's entire family was always in trouble with the law, so it was no wonder Melvin had been nabbed. As for Melvin, he promised to never ever break the law again, and he almost succeeded. Unfortunately, some of his hot rods were a bit too noisy and too fast, so he racked up a few speeding tickets in and around White Bear. In his defense, Melvin always maintained the tickets were "no big deal." According to him, he just got caught "enjoying some summertime fun." None of us could argue with that.

Shameless

The Nicklesons lived one block over and two blocks down on County Road F. Their house was nestled—well, more like half-buried—behind huge, ancient pine trees and a funky, half-finished, half-grossly-painted garage with garbage and garbage cans spewed all around it. Everything about the Nicklesons seemed to be a half-assed and half-baked attempt at propriety—that was how Mom and Howie described them. It was also a good thing that those big old pine trees and that funky half-finished garage helped hide Mrs. Nickleson, aka Dolores, from the neighbors' view. You see, Dolores liked to walk around butt-naked, strutting her stuff in front of the living-room picture window for all the world to see, to gawk at her large, flopping-balloon breasts and everything else below her waist, which was rarely or only barely covered by her dirty, tattered panties. Dolores in the buff put on a show for everyone, but she didn't seem to care. In fact, she seemed to flaunt it—and them—in her neighbors' prying eyes.

"If they don't like what they see, let them shut their own goddamn blinds." That was Dolores's philosophy, and Dolores epitomized the Nickleson clan's reputation: shameless.

Dolores was not only bold and bawdy, she was also nasty and mean. Her over-the-top foul language put her in a league of her own. She was the only woman I ever knew who could curse worse than my mom could. Besides her potty mouth, exhibitionist tendencies, and combative personality, Dolores was dirty—physically dirty. She regularly appeared from her kitchen charging like a buffalo in a rage with dried egg or cereal or ketchup on her lips and cheeks. The neighbor kids used to joke that anyone brave enough to kiss Dolores would receive a full meal of leftovers.

Mom and Howie knew all about the Nicklesons because the police were called to their house at least twice each season to settle a domestic dispute, and Howie was a policeman. Mom and Howie told me to stay away from them—all of them. They said that the Nicklesons' brood of dirty-faced kids had sprouted like weeds from the worst kind of seed—even though they did live on the same side of the tracks as we did. But the middle daughter, Danielle (nicknamed D), was in my grade, and we became neighborhood pals mostly because we both liked the same boys during grade school—and because she bathed regularly. Even still, Mom and Howie made me promise whenever I walked the streets in our neighborhood to visit D to be sure to get back home by dark—especially if it was a Friday night—not that the other nights were a whole lot tamer or safer. The Nicklesons got wild and crazy from all their drinking every night of the week, but Fridays meant the start of the weekend, and weekends for the Nicklesons were … well, let's just say they were sometimes beyond belief.

*****

D's father, who Mom always said was a "real piece of work," rarely made it home on Friday nights. In fact, sometimes he never made it home all weekend long. His name was Pewter Dan. No one seemed to know how he got his name, but he was half-Irish and half-Sioux, so maybe that had something to do with it. Monday through Friday, Pewter Dan worked at the St. Paul slaughterhouse (a gross place to work, for sure, which I figured was probably why he drank so much). Every Friday was payday, and as soon as Pewter Dan got paid, he would head to his favorite watering hole, a dive bar on Rice Street.

Early one Friday evening, D and I were sitting on her front steps talking about boys we liked and girls we couldn't stand when Dolores stormed out the front door, nearly tripping over both of us, yelling, "Where's that son of a bitch now? He should've been home an hour ago. I'm going to that goddamn bar and haul his sorry ass home, the dirty, no-good bum! He needs to be here to help me with you brats." (There were six Nickleson siblings.) "Danielle, you take care of your sisters and brothers. I'll be back in a few hours." Having issued that order, Dolores climbed in their rattletrap car and sped off down Floral Drive heading for St. Paul.

I looked at D and said, "There she goes again. I hope she doesn't kill him this time."

"Boy," D replied, "Mom sure had fire in her eyes this time, and she's super pissed because Dad has been drunk every night this week. He barely made it to work this morning. Most days he's *so* hung over, I don't know how he keeps his job. Yesterday, Mom told him to get his ass to work or he'd be a dead man for sure. So, off he staggered."

"I can't imagine working every day at a slaughterhouse where all those cows and pigs are killed and butchered," I said. "I can't even stand to think about it. Maybe that's why he drinks so much."

"Hell, his entire family drinks almost as much as he does—all his siblings and his parents. It's in their blood, their Irish-Indian blood. And most of them work at the slaughterhouse too."

"Are you worried you'll turn out the same?" I asked. "After all, you have the same blood."

"God, I hope not," D said. "I don't want to end up like either of my parents. Mom's crazy, and Dad's a drunk. Two beers is my limit from now on." I hoped she meant it.

It was getting dark now, and I knew I'd better get home fast before Mom got angry, so I left D sitting on the front steps and told her I'd call her in the morning.

*****

The next day, D called me before I could call her. "Patty, meet me halfway between our houses. You're never gonna believe what happened last night after you left."

"I'll be there in a second," I said, gulping the last of my breakfast and making sure to wipe the milk and cereal from around my mouth. (I sure didn't want to go out looking like gross Dolores.) Scurrying around the corner of the house, I saw D waiting for me down the street. "What happened?" I asked, eager to hear the details.

"Well," D said, "last night, Mom went to the bar, and when she didn't see Dad there, she asked the bartender where the hell he was. Rico, the bartender, being a pal of Dad's, at first said he hadn't seen him and didn't know where he was. Mom didn't believe him, so she slammed her beer bottle over his head, and he confessed. Even Rico fears her and for good reason. He knows what she's capable of doing.

"He told Mom, 'I think maybe I saw Pewter Dan go out the back door, right there behind you. You can check for yourself, Dolores.' So she did. She ran out the back door, slamming it hard behind her. And there he was, rolling around on the ground with some peroxide blonde who looked to be half his age. There they were, having sex, right there in an alley between the overflowing, smelly trash cans while an old, hungry cat perched on one of the dented lids and watched them. Mom started kicking his drunken ass and that bitch in the sides and anywhere else her foot landed, ignoring Miss Peroxide's screams. Mom has no pity. Meanwhile, Dad was yelling, 'Now, now, Dolores, it's not what you think. This lady came on to me. It's not my fault—honest. She made me do it. Stop kicking us, please! This bitch screws us all!'

"But Mom kept kicking and cursing until she wore herself out. Then she grabbed hold of him by his neck and dragged him out of the alley and across Rice Street, which by that time was heavy with weekend traffic and local passersby, all of whom witnessed the scene but didn't want to get involved since it was a private affair. Then she shoved him on to the backseat floor and drove home. He wasn't dead, but almost," D said as she finished her story.

I thought, Wow, maybe next time she'll really do it. But I didn't say that to D.

*****

The insanities of this ribald family continued for as long as I lived in Beartown. (White Bear was often called Beartown as we became hippy teenagers; it sounded more hip and cool to us.) I remember one hot, humid summer day, a couple of years later, when I walked into the Nicklesons' house through the side patio door that hung slightly off-kilter near that funky, half-finished garage. Their doors were never locked, and all of us neighbor kids came and went whenever we felt like it. We never stole their food because the food in the refrigerator, or even what was left on the stove, was always rotten and moldy green. It appeared to have sat there for weeks, dead bugs and all.

It was about noon, and as I made my way down the hall to D's room, I noticed Janelle, D's older sister. Janelle was seventeen, a high school dropout, and had already had an abortion—everybody knew this because nothing the Nicklesons ever did was a secret—and she was propped up against the wall by Ernie, the twelve-year-old, pimple-faced freak from across the street. Ernie had his pants down around his ankles. Janelle didn't have much on from what I could tell, and there they were screwing in the middle of the day for all the world to see. They both said hi as I walked past them to get to D's bedroom. They didn't stop and didn't seem to be the least bit embarrassed that I'd caught them in the act. That's when I realized what *shameless* really meant.

I opened D's bedroom door and asked her if she knew what her sister was doing. "Yeah," she said. "That kid comes over all the time. It's nothing. Janelle has been on birth control for almost a year, and she says she can have sex anytime and anywhere she likes. She doesn't care how old the boys are. Nothing I can do about it. Mom's never here, and Dad's always too far out of it to care."

"But Ernie's so ugly," I said. "What is she thinking?"

"She's not, Patty. She's not thinking about anyone but herself. She just loves to have sex—and she usually gets it three or four times a day."

The thought of that nearly made me sick. I wasn't sure I could look Janelle in the face again knowing now what she was really like. After that, I started to keep my distance from the Nicklesons' house. Janelle's reputation had spread around town, and soon boys of all ages—even the sixty-plus-year-old mailman—were lining up for a turn with her. No way could I tell Mom and Howie, or anyone else, what I had seen and heard. It was just too much to share with my more usual, upright friends. No, I had to keep this story to myself. It was my forever secret.

Five years later, Janelle married a Hell's Angel dude and moved out of state. Apparently she lived happily ever after with her biker husband and a brood of seven kids. D graduated from high school and eventually married a gorgeous, blonde Viking-looking guy who, aside from his very blonde hair, resembled the singer B.J. Thomas. They had two kids. Over time, D and I drifted apart, yet every five years or so, I'll get a phone call from her and we will laugh about our childhood days. She confided once that her handsome husband sometimes frequented the same bar on Rice

97

Street where her dad hung out and that she often had to go in there and haul his ass home—even after she caught him with his pants down in the alleyway, just like her dad.

So, I guess the Nickleson saga continues. I feel sorry for D. She was the best of the bunch, but I have learned to steer clear of people who are that crazy and *shameless*—even if, as my parents said, they do live on the same side of the tracks as we do.

Candy Striping

At sixteen, all of us kids had jobs. That was because once we turned fifteen, to keep living under our mom's roof, we needed to start paying rent, rent being a minimum of fifty dollars each per month. Mom said times were hard, especially because of the huge debt that Bruce left her to deal with. Bruce did not pay his bills, so all us kids pitched in and helped Mom get out of debt.

Before my first job, as a soda jerk at Reeds Drug Store, Johnny and I had volunteer jobs as candy stripers at Regions Hospital in St. Paul. I was fourteen, and Johnny was sixteen. I think Mom wanted to teach us kids something, but what that was, was unclear. What could we learn from being around sick and dying people or from people recovering from some horrible surgery? We were about to find out.

During the '60s, only girls were allowed to apply to volunteer as candy stripers, so Johnny, in his usual fashion, posed as a girl and wore one of my dresses. He told the staff lady his name was Jackie. The hospital staff lady handed us our outfits, which were these red-and-white jumpers that were kind of cute—especially on Jackie. We both were accepted and spent every Sunday for one summer at the hospital, feeding the sick and delivering medicine, mail, and flowers to various people with various ailments.

One day, as we were attending to a very old lady, Jackie was told to feed her as I was there straightening up her side table and bed linens. This lady took a couple bites of Jell-O without any trouble, but on the third bite, she bit down on the spoon and with a huge sigh, dropped over dead right on the spot—at least that is what we thought and felt. With wide eyes, Jackie looked at me in horror and disbelief and whispered, "Let's get out of here. This old lady is dead. The spoon is stuck in her mouth." To this, I replied, "We better call a nurse to be sure. Maybe she just didn't like that Jell-O, or maybe she had an allergic reaction and fainted." Jackie agreed as I pressed the button on the wall for help. A nurse showed up within minutes and confirmed that this old broad was dead. We were told we could go home for the day. Hallelujah! One dead feeding was plenty for us for the day!

We went home where Jackie went back to being Johnny, and we told Mom and Howie all about the events of our day. Mom said, "Now that is a great lesson for you kids. You have now seen death up close and know what it is like. I am proud of you both. Dinner's ready; we're having your favorite, chicken and dumplings."

Life went back to normal. That fall was the end of our experience as candy stripers. Good thing as it was time for both of us to get paying jobs to stay under Mom's roof. We gladly did just that.

Feeding the Fishermen

Yes, it was true. As soon as we turned fifteen, Mom expected all of us kids to pay a minimum of fifty dollars a month to live under her roof. None of us was willing to argue with Mom. She made the rules and we obeyed—most of the time. Shortly after our adventure as candy stripers, Mom came home one afternoon and announced, "I saw Darrell, down at Reed's Drug yesterday, and he said he's hiring. Patricia, get your butt down there and apply for a job. Put your tennis shoes on, and walk down there right now. He said he is working nine to five this week and will hire the first few kids that show up."

No way was I about to argue with Mom on this subject, but I couldn't help but say, "How am I supposed to work and go to school too?" To which she replied, "Honey, you are strong and have enough energy and drive to do both. Now, put your shoes on and get going." So I did, and a week later, I started working in my free time at White Bear's only drug store, starting in the back as cook and dishwasher, and then moving up front as soda jerk.

Why they called us soda jerks I'll never know. We (me and another older girl from my school, named Jane) were not jerks at all. What we really were, after a few days of on-the-job training, were cooks, bakers, malt and sundae makers, and anything else that pertained to the operation of a full kitchen under the watchful eye of Ms. Gerda Steffenhauser, our very German bossy boss. She had us working nonstop from the time we arrived until (sometimes) hours after our shift ended, making a multitude of flavored malted milks (mostly chocolate and vanilla), banana splits, cherry and lime Cokes, and all kinds of phosphate drinks. If we worked the morning shift, we cooked breakfasts—lots of breakfasts, made-to-order breakfasts for the rough-and-tough fishermen who ate there each and every day before heading out onto White Bear Lake, the best lake to fish for the largest trout or walleye possible. They didn't have to walk far—the lake was only two hundred feet (or so it seemed) in front Reed's Drug Store, on the other side of the parking lot.

These fishermen soon took a liking to me. Apparently, I got pretty darn good at frying their eggs just the way they asked me. They always congregated in groups of at least three or four. They were bearded and burly middle-aged types who sat at the counter stools and joked about all the latest news around town, spreading more wicked rumors faster than any of the waspy women's tongues.

One day, while waiting for the toaster to pop up their white toast to butter, I said, "Hey Charlie, you gossip worse than any of my girlfriends. Bet your wife gets sick of hearing all your crap."

Charlie quickly replied, "Patty, Patty, my little wife loves me, all three hundred pounds of me. What grade are you in, young lady?"

"Ninth grade."

He said, "Bet you get good grades young lady," and I replied, "Average in most subjects accept for physical education. I get all A's in that because I love to run, jump hurdles, and play most sports." At that, Charlie's buddy said, "I bet you do."

Little did I know, as Gerda told me later, that these men were huge flirts and loved sitting there each morning, asking all kinds of questions, for no good reason at all, but my tips were great! I figured it was mostly because of those eggs, but later, I wondered if it wasn't for the cheap thrills they got from goading me on.

Whatever … I was okay with it because this job not only allowed me to help Mom with the grocery bills, but it also afforded me the opportunity to buy my very first very little emerald ring, with a beautiful real diamond on one side of the emerald setting. This ring, my first expensive thing ever, I bought from the one and only jewelry store in White Bear my senior year in high school. Believe it or not, I continued to work at Reed's Drug Store until I graduated.

By the time I did graduate, I had managed to get a few raises and even moved up to head cashier by my senior year. I also managed to maintain my average grades. They weren't great, but they were good enough to get by. All in all, I couldn't complain and was even a bit pleased with myself for having the ambition to attend my classes (most of them) and work the entire time. Mom and Howie were proud of my accomplishments, and life in White Bear was good.

PART V
COMING OF AGE IN WHITE BEAR LAKE

Wild Times at White Bear High

No doubt about it, I was a social butterfly in high school, flitting here and there, and fluttering my eyelashes at all the guys, I was what some called, way back then, a free spirit. I did things most of the goody-two-shoes didn't dare do and hung with those kids who felt and acted the same. We weren't exactly the worst kids in the school, just a little challenging, so to speak. We pushed the edge of the envelope time and again, and eventually, paid for our behavior if or when we got caught.

My sophomore year was fairly quiet—well, actually, more like boring. I attended most of my classes without any major incidents, but every now and then, I'd give myself permission to take an AWOL break to enjoy a nice swim at county beach. I usually had my swimsuit in my purse during the warmer months, and the beach was only about a half mile away. Since I loved to run, I could easily sneak away between classes, sprint to the lake, enjoy a refreshing dip, and get back to school before being missed. I usually timed my return just as the bell rang so I could quickly blend in with the rushing masses in the hallways.

However, one day as I was trying to slip in unnoticed after one of these self-justified breakouts, the bug-eyed hall monitor, Mrs. Longfellow, was standing guard inside the front door.

"Young lady, where in the hell have you been?" she bellowed, blocking my path with her fullback-sized body.

"Oh! I'm sorry Mrs. Longfellow," I said. "It was so hot in my math class, I had to go to the beach to cool off."

She replied, "Patty, follow me to the principal's office."

I pleaded, "Please, Mrs. Longfellow, don't call my Mom. She'll kill me. Please let me go to my next class. I promise I'll behave."

She gazed at me with disbelief and said, "Only this time. I'm too busy to mess with your bullshit anyway, so be on your way. I don't want to catch you sneaking out again! You hear?"

"Yes, I promise. Thank you, thank you, Mrs. Longfellow," I said as I turned and hurried to my next class, heaving a sigh of relief as I scurried away.

*****

My sophomore class had seven hundred students, which meant that for Mrs. Longfellow to catch all of us at our pranks and games, she would certainly have to stay on her toes. We often pressed our luck, and she'd chase us down—or at least try to. It was a game, like cat and mouse. It made school fun.

About a month after this close call, a few of my girlfriends from homemaking class decided we didn't really need to know how to make a Baked Alaska and that it was much too nice a day outside to be cooped up in school. Joyce said, "Hey, I have my parents' station wagon; let's go to Apple River and go inner-tubing. We can pick up McDonald's on the way."

Jean, Kay, Deb, and I looked at each other and, nodding in agreement, began planning how we could leave without being noticed. We were sneaky and good at not getting caught, most of the time. After some discussion, we decided to leave during lunch hour, a time when students were allowed to eat lunch outside on picnic benches and hang out on the lawn.

We had just gathered on the lawn when Kay said, "Don't turn around, Patty; Mrs. Longfellow is standing right by the side door. It looks as if she has her eye on someone smoking in the parking lot. How about we go around to the other side of the building and sneak off? This is our chance." We managed our escape by crouching down behind all the cars, inching our way to Joyce's car, quietly creeping in, and gently shutting the doors. Just as the bell rang, Joyce gunned the engine, and we were off for a fun day on the river.

Little did we know that Joyce had also stolen a bottle of Boone's Farm apple wine from her parents' liquor cabinet that morning. She pulled it out from under the front seat as soon as we were out of Mrs. Longfellow's guided-radar vision. We chugged and drank our way to the river, eating our burgers and fries, and laughing our heads off (as girls will do) over nothing and everything. We drove with all the windows down and the FM rock channel on full blast, listening to The Doors, The Beatles, Joe Cocker, and all the other rock stars of the day. We enjoyed a glorious, sunny day frolicking in the Apple River, getting a little drunk, and turning various shades of pink and red from the sun. We made it home just in time for supper—with no problems, having covered up our sunburns with sweatshirts.

The next morning (a Friday, thank God), as each of us arrived at school on our various buses, Mrs. Longfellow was waiting for us. She greeted us as if we were her most favorite girls in the whole school and told us to please sit on the benches by the front steps. She had that bug-eyed, sly smirk on her face that always gave me the creeps (and the others too, I'm sure). She had no way of proving that we had skipped our afternoon classes the day before (the teachers had too many kids to count or keep track of), but we all knew she was on to us. Through her smirky grin, she said, "Girls, nice sunburn. How in the hell did you get so burnt since yesterday?"

Deb answered with all due respect, "Good morning, Mrs. Longfellow. You look very nice today. We hit the beach right after school yesterday. Wasn't it a beautiful day?"

Mrs. Longfellow gave each of us that special bug-eyed look that said she didn't believe a word of it, and then said, "Get to class. The bell just rang."

We all fled to our classes, safe for now from Mrs. Longfellow's wrath. Afterwards, I had the feeling she sort of respected our tenacity to take chances and had probably acted the same way at our age. It was as if she had caught us because she had "been there and done that." Her smirk gave her away.

*****

Another memorable run-in with Mrs. Longfellow happened after I had started dating Tim, who just happened to be the best-looking guy in our high school; he had long, glowing black hair and a super-great body, four inches taller than my forever five-foot-four frame. He was also the kind of boy that had it all going for him. He was good in all sports (especially football and hockey) and got above average grades. Many of the cuter girls, as well as some not so cute, chased him like wildcats hoping he would fall for them, but it didn't happen. This year, he was mine, and that was just fine by me.

We had been dating for over a month, and things were getting serious—meaning that he would and did beat up any other boy that glanced at me. (His fighting was good practice—or so we all thought—since he was the quarterback for the WBHS football team and needed to be tough.) One morning before school, Tim asked me if I wanted to ride to Forest Lake during lunch break in his dazzling 1955 aqua and white Chevy that all the boys were envious of because it was a classic in mint condition.

Of course, I said, "Yes! I'd love to go for a drive with you during lunch." This time, we sneaked out as soon as the lunch bell rang, making our way through the hallways thick with kids pushing and shoving their way toward the outside lawn. Slipping out the side door, we slithered our way to his car, which he had parked behind a row of thick bushes. Jumping in the front seat and snuggling close together, off we went with the windows rolled down and music blasting. On our way to Forest Lake, we stopped at the A&W drive-through and ordered cheeseburgers, fries, and root beer, making out while we ate. In the thrill of the moment, he said he thought he loved me, and I said I thought the same. After finishing our lunch, we drove back to White Bear, thinking we could easily sneak back in the same way we had snuck out, but it wasn't to be.

Tim parked his Chevy in the same spot behind the bushes, and then we crept to the side door only to find it was locked. Not good! We had no choice but to crawl—so we wouldn't be seen by kids in each class that we passed—all the way around to the front entrance. And who was there to meet us? None other than the infamous Mrs. Longfellow, standing guard with her regular stance, arms crossed in front of her. Apparently, Tim's loud muffler had given us away. She towered over us as we stood up wiping the grass stains from our kneecaps and brushing away the dirt. "Well, well, well, if it isn't the lovers. Where in the hell have you been?" she yelled in our faces.

Tim cleared his throat (as if that gave him a feeling of confidence—it appeared to at least help the situation because he was one of the most popular jocks, which, it seemed, Mrs. Longfellow was proud of) and said, "Good afternoon, Mrs. Longfellow. We are so sorry to be late. I took Patty to lunch, and there was a really, really long train we had to wait for on our way back."

"Uh huh, uh huh. How come I didn't hear any train?" she asked.

"I'm not sure, Mrs. Longfellow. The mid-day train came through town early today. You were probably busy with other kids and didn't hear the whistle."

Knowing that no damn train ran through town at this hour, Mrs. Longfellow stared at us with her bug-eyed smirk and said, "Tim, that is a boldface lie, but I'll give you an A+ for making up a pretty darn good story for wherever the hell you two were. Now get to your classes!" she growled as she turned and walked away. And that was that. That day, I finally realized Mrs. Longfellow was mostly full of hot air.

*****

During the rest of my high school years, I had a few more snarky encounters with Mrs. Longfellow, but for the most part, I stayed out of trouble. With all my good friends and occasional boyfriends (I had three more main boyfriends after Tim,) high school was pretty much a breeze. My grades in most subjects were average except for my English and P.E. classes—I aced them with little effort. Mom was super pleased when I graduated with my class because I was the first female in our family to do so. I was proud that she was pleased, and I often wondered if she had known just how easy (and tons of fun) it really was.

Sauna Parties:
Another Wacky Winter
Pastime

Almost everyone I knew when I was growing up got a case of cabin fever at some point during the long, dark days of our Minnesota winters, so the Looney Latooneys weren't the only ones who dreamed up wacky ways to amuse themselves and enjoy the sub-zero temperatures. I had a large number of friends in White Bear who claimed Swedish, Norwegian, or some other Scandinavian descent. One of the pastimes these folks most enjoyed, even on the coldest days of winter, was sitting and sweating in their cute, little, outdoor wooden cubicles called saunas. This was a particularly popular pastime after the Christmas holidays, because everyone claimed we could sweat away those extra pounds that we customarily gained from exercising less and eating more of our mothers' butter-rich pastries and tummy-warming homemade breads and stews.

Anyway, there was a ritual to this sauna stuff. First, you were expected to sit naked (or, if you were with co-ed friends, you could wear your cutest swimsuit) in this square box of a building that somehow filled up with hot steam. Then, when you were sufficiently "sweated out," much like a plump piece of kielbasa, you were expected to dash out the door, dive into the closest snow bank, and roll around until you were what could best be called freeze-dried. After that, you'd hustle your numb buns into a refreshing shower to warm up your physically shocked system back to a somewhat normal state. At least, that's how it was supposed to work.

Sauna parties were popular when I was in high school, and one of my favorite hosts was Red Swensen, one of my new ninth-grade friends. Red's parents owned one of the grandest homes on the north side of White Bear Lake. They not only had the newest and best outdoor sauna, but their home also boasted six indoor showers to accommodate all the guests who came to enjoy this rather crazy custom. Red must have thought I was really into this sweating stuff since this was the fourth time I'd been invited to sauna with him. On this particular day, I brought my girlfriend Germaine with me. Red greeted us at the front door and said, "Hurry up girls, I've got the sauna all steamed up."

Germaine and I retreated to one of the spacious spare bedrooms where we changed into our cutest and skimpiest bikinis, and then we wrapped ourselves up in the Swenson's oversized and expensive towels, and tip-toed (barefoot of course) across an snow-crusted expanse of lawn and climbed into the foggy sauna. Dropping our towels, we took our seats and waited for the fat to start melting away. After what seemed to be way too long (I had begun to feel like a candle dripping wax), Red, the Nordic Viking, said, "Let's go jump in the snow. I've had enough of this for now."

Yeah! At last, I thought. So, we jumped up and ran out, rolling and tumbling around in the snowdrifts. When we were all breathing harder than seemed humanly possible, we made a mad dash across the backyard to hit the showers.

The Swenson's shower room was quite impressive. Each of the six shower enclosures was adorned with an ornately decorated glass door. The three of us quickly jumped into one of the showers, and I heard Red yell, "Don't put the water on too hot. It will shock your body too much, so be careful."

I figured he was talking to Germaine. After all, I knew the routine. This was my fourth time here. I set the temperature to medium warm and stepped under the cascading waterfall. It felt great. I felt great, but then my head started spinning. I felt as if I was on one of those carnival rides that spins you around and around, and then I fainted, crashing right through that fancy glass shower door and landing like a rock on the Swenson's very plush aqua carpet. I was out and down for the count. Thank God for that carpet. It helped cushion my fall. Red and Germaine ran to my side and shook me like a rag doll to wake me up. When I came to, all I could say was, "Where am I? What happened?"

Red grabbed a hand towel and began to wipe up the blood that was gushing from my arm. I had fallen on my right side when I crashed through the door, leaving me with a large gash on my right forearm. Before long, Mom appeared (apparently Red's mother had called her) and said, "Oh, my goodness! What happened here?"

"I think she must have fainted," Red said. "All we heard was a loud *thud* and the sound of breaking glass. Then we saw her lying on the carpet. Patty cut her arm when she fell, so I wrapped it up tight with a towel to stop the bleeding."

"Thank you, dear. That was smart thinking," Mom said as she helped me get dressed. Our next stop was Dr. Rand's office where I got a few stitches in my arm to close the gash.

After we finally got home, Mom said, "Honey, before you ever do this again, make sure you eat something solid. You don't need to sweat off any fat. You're skinny enough the way you are."

"What?" I replied. "I'm not so sure, Mom. I think this happened because the sauna was extra hot and my body went into some kind of shock. But, don't worry. I think I'll lay off this sauna thing for a while." At least Mom wasn't mad at me, and that was a big relief.

Anyway, that was not only my last sauna experience for a good long time, but also my last fainting spell for a good long time. Thank goodness!

Skinny-Dipping

Skinny-dipping. Who doesn't love doing that? It was a favorite pastime of mine during my teen years, and I enjoyed it any chance I got. Usually, I was with a small group of girlfriends and guy friends, although sometimes a boyfriend got thrown into the mix, too. Most often, we'd head to Bellaire Beach (unless a closer beach was nearby when the idea struck). We'd gather right around dusk, drink a few beers in the parking lot, and then walk down the narrow path to the beach, stripping off articles of clothing as we approached the shoreline. Nine times out of ten, we got in and out and away with little if any notice, but there was that one time we got thoroughly busted by the cops. Here's what happened.

One warm, glorious summer night, Jean, Paco, Richard, Kay, and I were hanging out at Bellaire Beach. Paco had scored a little weed, so we smoked a couple joints and drank a couple beers, enjoying the sense of freedom we felt lying beneath the brilliant starlight of the northern Minnesota sky. It was, by all measures, a perfect evening … that is, until, Kay yelled, "Last one in is a rotten egg!" The next thing we knew, she stripped down completely, which of course meant that the rest of us had to do the same.

The pot had already made us silly and loud. Paco was singing at the top of his lungs as we peeled off our clothes and ran into the lake, swimming and singing our way toward the large, square dock anchored about a hundred yards away. Pulling ourselves onto the dock, we rolled around on top laughing our heads off while still singing songs by the Beatles and Rolling Stones—our favorite rock-and-roll tunes of the time. We were having a great time belly flopping, cannon balling, and diving off each side of the dock, all the while laughing, joking around, and singing like wannabe rock stars.

It seemed like no time at all, but I guess we'd been out there quite some time before we saw what looked like a cop car slowly inching its way down the beach road to the shoreline. At this point, we were happy to have the dock to hide behind as the cop turned on his spotlight and aimed it in our direction. With his bullhorn blasting, he said, "Okay, kids, come out. You're causing too much commotion, and the neighbors are complaining."

We simultaneously thought, "Come out! Is he crazy?" How were we going to do that when we first had to swim back to the beach and then give away the fact that we'd been skinny-dipping? How embarrassing! At least, by then, it was pitch black outside, and there was no moon to light up our bare behinds—nothing more illuminating than those magnificent stars casting glimmering shadows upon our nakedness.

The cop, however, seemed to be getting impatient. He got back on his loudspeaker and said, "Come out, *now*! I'm going to wait *here* until you do." We couldn't see that far in the darkness, but we knew he was standing guard next to our path of scattered clothes, which meant he was already aware of our predicament.

"Oh, God!" That's what we all felt at this point.

Finally, Richard said, "We better do as he says. We'll be in more trouble if we don't. Besides, it's getting cold out here. There's no way we can stay on this dock all night, and it sure doesn't look like he's planning on leaving any time soon."

I knew the cop's voice was familiar, but it took a while for it to register in my mind. At last, I heard myself whispering, with a sense of doom and dread, "Oh my God! That cop is Jerry Sandler. He's a good friend of my stepdad. When Howie gets wind of this, he's going to either die laughing or kill me. I am in so much trouble already. Let's swim ashore and get this over with."

So, that's exactly what we did. As we tiptoed out of the water, baring our naked bodies for all the world to see, Jerry kindly turned off his spotlight. We stumbled about, still giggling, while digging through a pile of helter-skelter belongings, searching for our own clothing to put on before Jerry blew the whistle on us again. We hustled as best we could, and about the time we were half-dressed, Jerry came walking closer toward us, with a saunter that suggested he must have been grinning hugely and enjoying every minute of our discontent. No doubt, he was also thinking how much he wished he could have joined us in this warm summer evening escapade. (At least, that's my take on the situation.) Plus, he was a cute cop, but that was beside the point—at least right now … under these circumstances.

Jerry had recognized me right off and said, "Hi, Patty. You and your friends were way too loud out there tonight. I have to issue you guys a warning ticket. I have no choice. Here Patty, take this warning ticket—it's for all of you. You'll have to appear in court and plead your case to the judge. If you're lucky, it'll be Judge Perry. He'll probably find all this amusing and let you all go scot-free. If not, you may have to pay a small fine. Either way, you have to appear in court on the date stated on your ticket. Good night, kids. Now, go home."

Jerry left and we got back into Paco's car feeling a bit sick in our guts, thinking that we would all have to appear in court and plead our case, our case being that it was a warm summer night and we were having innocent fun at the beach. I looked at the ticket and read the date for our court appearance, which was to be the following Tuesday at nine a.m. Paco, Richard, Jean, and Kay all agreed that we would meet there at the appointed time and get this over with as quickly as possible. But first, we had to go home and face our parents.

I was certain Howie had already been notified of this current fiasco, so when I arrived home, around eleven thirty, I wasn't surprised to find him waiting for me. He had just gotten off his night shift and was sitting at the kitchen table when I walked through the back door.

"It looks like you kids were having a bit too much fun tonight, dear." He spoke with no hint of emotion. "Next time, remember to keep the noise down. Now, go to bed. We'll talk in the morning."

"Are we in trouble?" I asked. "What will happen when we go to court next week?"

"If you're lucky, Judge Perry will be working, and he'll most likely let you walk. Now, go to bed. We'll deal with this tomorrow." So, that's precisely what I did. I went to bed hoping this entire evening would be nothing more than a bad dream by morning.

On Sunday morning, when I crawled out of my room for breakfast, Mom and Howie seemed to be in a nice, quiet, pleasant mood. I wondered if I were still dreaming, but proceeded to get some cereal out of the cupboard and pour it into a bowl. As I sat down to top it with some milk, Mom said, "Hmm, what did you kids do last night, Patty? Sounds like you had a wee bit too much fun at the beach."

"Yes, Mom," I replied. "We were having a lot of fun until Jerry showed up with his spotlight. Why did he have to ticket us? We weren't being rowdy or anything."

Mom said, "Honey, don't you know who lives in that big house next to the beach? That's Mrs. Pugh, the old widow who's always stirring things up with our city council and police staff. She's that crab who likes to get teens in trouble and who always calls the cops if there's even the slightest noise around the lake. But, don't worry. Howie may be able to put a word in for you kids before Tuesday."

Tuesday came faster than I had anticipated. The plan was for the five us to meet at the White Bear courthouse at eight thirty sharp. I arrived at eight twenty-five. Paco was already there sitting on the bench near the entrance. As I sat down next to him, he said, "Let's hope we get in and out of here quickly, and without a fine. I only have a twenty in my wallet if we need to pay something. I hope that'll be enough. When this is over, let's all go to Big Ben for breakfast. What do you think?"

No doubt about it, Paco was nervous. "Yeah, Paco," I said, "That sounds like a plan. Think positive—oh, here comes Kay, Jean, and Richard. Kay, put that cigarette out!" I shouted. "It doesn't look good for us to be seen smoking here."

"Yeah, yeah," Kay said, stomping out the crimson butt.

"It's time," I said. "Let's get this over with."

We entered the courthouse and proceeded to find our way into the one and only courtroom. There were only about twenty people scattered about. We took our seats in what appeared to be the audience section and held our breath as a bailiff called, "All rise."

To our relief, a big fat judge by the name of Perry was presiding this morning. I remember thinking that we were in luck. Leaning over to Jean, I whispered, "Check it out, his name plate. It's Judge Perry. We may get out of here without having to pay a fine."

The charge against us was defined as disturbing the peace and indecency on a public beach.

Judge Perry, in his most legalistic voice, intoned, "The case of Patty and friends, please approach the bench." He gave us a dead serious look as we walked forward and then burst out laughing.

"You kids need to learn to be a bit quieter at that beach. Mrs. Pugh will call us each and every time she hears something out of the ordinary. She lives in that oversized, garish mansion right next to Bellaire Beach. Next time, if you want to go skinny-dipping, go to the County Beach ... or even White Bear Beach. But still, try to be quiet. At least, do your best to pipe down and try not to disturb the neighbors. There are a lot of old fogies who rent homes along the beach roads—all around the lake. Those old farts go to bed by nine. Don't disturb them, and you'll stay out of trouble. Now, get out of here! I don't want to see any of you in here again all summer!"

We each said thank you to Judge Perry and left the courthouse to enjoy a celebratory breakfast at Big Ben. We all knew we had lucked out this time, and we were grateful for not having to pay a fine. When we walked into the restaurant, Howie, Jerry, and Bill (the cutest cop of all) were sitting at the counter having their mid-morning cup of joe and slice of freshly baked pie. Howie nodded in my direction, winked, and waved. That said it all. He knew we were only having innocent fun on a hot summer evening, and it was only because a crabby old lady had squealed that we had to go through all this trouble. Summer continued with no more courtroom appearances from any of us. We learned to keep the volume down while at the beach, even though we continued to test our limits in other areas of our lives. All in all, however, life that summer was grand.

My BFF Jean

In the seventh grade, I met my very best forever friend. Her name was Jean, and she looked like me, dressed like me, and liked most of the same things as me. We both had shiny blonde hair all the way down to our waists, cut straight across at the ends, and parted down the middle (as was the fashion of the day). Her hair was pearly white, while mine was more corn-silk yellow. Our complexions were similar too. Her face was pale white, mine pink white. A lot of people got us confused, and some even thought we were twins. How silly! Jean was Norwegian. I'm Polish, mostly.

There were differences between us, especially when it came to sports and school. I was crazy about sports and excelled at anything that involved running: softball, tennis, track, and hockey. Because of my flexibility and agility, I also did well in gymnastics. However, even though I was always a highly competitive athlete, I was just an average student. Jean, on the other hand, hated all sports, but enjoyed math and science, neither of which were my better subjects. When Jean heard I was the first pick for the girls' hockey team, she said, "Hockey? Isn't that for boys?" I replied, "No way! Girls can play it just as well as guys. I'll show you." Later that year, I proved to her, our parents, and the entire class just how good I was at hockey by scoring the winning point for our grade. Mom was really proud of me, and even my big brother Mel gave me a huge hug for my accomplishment. Johnny, however, was indifferent, since he, like Jean, could not have cared less about any sporting activity.

I figured Jean didn't like sports because she had never been encouraged to play any of them. That's because Jean's parents were classy, upscale, small-town business people. They were always sweet, loving, and kind to Jean and me (not at all like some of my other friends' parents), but they appeared to be as old as most grandparents. Jean's mom, Edith, had long hair that she wore twisted up into a flat bun fastened to her head with a large brocade clip. She and her husband, Maynard, owned a gift shop in uptown White Bear that was stuffed full of beautiful, exotic, and expensive knick-knacks and fancy glass vases and figurines imported from all over the world. They even sold foreign chocolate bars in cocoa and cherry flavors. It was the nicest gift store in town, and Mr. and Mrs. Olson were liked and respected by everyone in White Bear. When she wasn't busy at the store, Edith made us delicate, lacy cookies, and she even taught me a few words in Norwegian. Most were quick little sayings I could use in any casual conversation, but I also picked up some other things I could whisper under my breath when necessary.

From the seventh grade on, Jean and I were inseparable. Sometimes after school we'd go to her house and hang out in the basement rec room where we'd dance and sing to the Supremes, pretending we were singing into hand mikes (using hand mirrors for the fake microphones). We shared even more good times when we'd sleep over at either her house or mine. We never slept much, though. Instead, we'd spend the entire night talking, laughing, and eating.

One time, we stole makeup from Edith's cosmetic bag and went to school wearing lipstick and eye shadow, which was totally forbidden back then. We were also notorious for wearing the shortest mini-skirts seen in town. On one particular day, we both pranced into school wearing the matching mini-skirts that I had sewn just for us. But before we got to our first-period class, we were swiftly cornered by the long boney arm of Mr. Thorn, the bumpy-nosed, bone thin, older-than-dirt hall monitor, who ordered us to go home and put on longer skirts (even though we often saw him glancing at all of us girls prancing about in those mini-skirts). He was probably following direct orders of the junior high school principal. This, of course, was before girls were allowed to wear pants to school and before blue jeans became my favorite article of clothing.

Around the age of fifteen, we tried smoking our first cigarettes … Marlboros. We were hanging out at Jean's house and evidently couldn't think of anything better to do with our time. "Want a cigarette?" she said, as she lit one up for each of us. Taking in a long draw of smoke, I thought, This is alright, but then, as we headed downstairs to the basement to play a new record by this new group from England called the Beatles, I all of a sudden felt really light-headed and then passed out, tumbling from the middle step to the bottom landing.

Thank God for carpeted stairs, because I didn't appear to be hurt from the fall. Standing up, I said, "Oh my God, that was scary! No more cigarettes for me."

Jean asked, "Are you sure you're okay?"

"Yeah, I'm okay, but you can keep those cigarettes. I'm done with smoking."

I only wish I had stayed scared longer. The very next weekend, we tried smoking again, and this time, it was easier. (At least, I didn't fall down the basement stairs again.) From that day on, Jean and I continued to smoke, enjoying it very much, thinking it made us look cool and sophisticated to the boys who were always hanging around Jean's house trying to get up close and personal with her older sister, Annie.

The Olsons were nice people, but Jean had one big problem with her parents: They were gone a lot, traveling all over the world buying new things for their home and gift shop. That meant Jean had to fend for herself most of the time, so she learned early on how to cook, bake, and handle any household problems that came up while they were away on one of their trips. Annie was supposed to be in charge, but she was no help around the house. She didn't clean, cook, or take any interest in anything much, other than the older boys who were always lurking around behind the tall bushes waiting for her, the girl with the largest breasts in White Bear Lake High, to come outside so they could stare at her huge boobs and try to get close enough to touch them. Annie was also a bit unfriendly toward me. I never knew why, but I didn't let that affect my friendship with Jean. My feeling was that Anne preferred the attention of her admirers and couldn't be bothered with her little sister or her friends.

Annie was fifteen when I met Jean, three years older than we were and the same age as my brother Mel. He probably knew all about her because there was bad gossip everywhere about Miss Annie. At that age, she was fully developed and was known miles around as the girl with the biggest breasts in town. To me, they were kind of gross, and I just hoped and prayed that Jean's wouldn't get that big. But a year later, they did. Jean was as top heavy as Annie, which made her the talk of our class. All the boys were now more interested in Jean than me, or so it appeared.

At first, this bothered me, but after a while, I noticed that those boys were not my type anyway. I preferred guys who liked me because I was great at sports and average otherwise. I was happy with my slow-to-develop bra size because, as a runner, my boobs needed to stay in place and not jiggle all around or bounce up and down. I was okay with my size. I wasn't really jealous because I thought Jean's and Annie's breasts were way too big and that someday they would probably have problems finding bras large enough to fit. I was right. They did.

Because their parents traveled so much, large parties, where lots of hanky-panky happened freely, were held regularly during their absence. One time, there were at least ten boys and maybe six girls grooving to the music of The Monkeys or The Kinks blasting from the stereo. Everyone was kissing and necking, and there were a few closed bedrooms where more went on—but not with me, though—not yet. I was just into necking until I went home one night with a hickey on my neck. My brothers mocked me for days when they saw it. I was embarrassed, and Mom was mad, so that stopped me for a while from going any farther or all the way with anyone.

Apparently, Edith and Maynard never caught on since their neighbors never talked about what was happening in their lovely upscale home while they were gone. I thought it was probably because they were mostly Methodists. However, the Olsons eventually suffered a bit of public humiliation as Annie got herself in trouble. All the kids knew that Annie was "fast"—otherwise known as easy. It could have happened at their home when Edith and Maynard were traveling overseas, but the local gossip was that it happened behind a bush near the school during lunch break. Only Annie and the boy knew for sure, and they weren't telling.

Annie had to drop out of school before her senior year and left town to have the baby, her first of four more to come. The boyfriend also left town, but he went in another direction. Annie was not seen again for a few years after that, but Jean told me she had called and that Annie was now married and happy. She was living near Hibbing with her husband, who worked at the Mesabi Iron Ore Range, and everything was just fine. Jean said that her mom and dad had had felt a great deal of embarrassment and shame about Annie's predicament. They never expected this to happen to their daughter, but life went on, at least for Edith, Maynard, and Annie.

My Second BFF Kay

Kay was my other best friend. I met her the summer after seventh grade. Kay was Irish. She had natural flaming-red hair and a face polka-dotted with freckles. She was chubby—no, she was more than chubby. Kay was fat. She was also serious and bold. I think she had to be serious and bold to live with her family. Here's how we met.

It was a hot, humid summer day, and I was at White Bear Beach swimming, sunning, and flirting with the boys. She came over to where I was sunbathing and said, "Hi, I'm Kay. Weren't you in my P.E class last year? Aren't you the one who took first place in the five-hundred-yard dash?"

I was impressed that she remembered me, so I said, "Yes, that was me. Nice to meet you. Why don't you get your towel and join me. This is a perfect day for sunbathing."

Kay set her towel down next to mine and rubbed baby oil with iodine all over her rather ample body. I said, "I bet you burn easy with all those freckles!"

"Sure do," Kay answered. "I have to be really careful, or I'll blister real bad."

"Well, let's just lie here a few minutes and then take a swim," I said. "Kenny, that cute lifeguard, is on duty, and his twin brother is somewhere around. Do you know them? They are both *so* cute."

Kay didn't answer. Perhaps she wasn't into beach boys with bleached blonde hair, but it didn't matter. We spent the rest of the day together enjoying each other's company. Kay talked a lot about her family that day. I learned she had two sisters and three brothers. She also mentioned that her mom was a witch—a good kind of witch, she said, one who could cast spells on anyone, anywhere. I thought that this talent might come in handy at some point.

When Mom found out about my new friend, she wasn't happy. She said Kay's family lived on the other side of the tracks, which, for some strange reason, was supposed to be a bad thing. I didn't understand this idea at all. How can one side of a railroad track make a person right or wrong, good or bad, evil or not evil? Anyway, the other side of the tracks was only three miles from where we lived. The homes were older there, more square (not like the rambler designs on Floral Drive), and they had larger yards, mostly without fences. Beyond that, I couldn't see much difference between their side and ours.

Once summer was over and we were back in school, I realized that Kay was a smart kid, almost too smart. She was so smart that most of the boys didn't talk to her. They were probably jealous. It appeared that boys our age didn't like to be threatened by overly smart girls. Good thing I was average. The other noteworthy thing about Kay is that she, like Jean and Johnny, didn't really like sports, or at least that's what she said. Usually, no one picked her to play on the softball team or any other team. Worse yet, if she was picked, she was the last one chosen for whatever sport we were practicing at the time. She didn't seem to mind, but I would have been pissed. I never said anything, but I guessed that no one picked her because she was fat and couldn't run fast. Anyway, we stayed friends forever--at least, almost forever.

Later on, I learned that there was a lot more to the whole story of her mom being a witch. She was also crazy, crazy in the worst kind of way. Her mom was schizophrenic. I didn't know what that was, but I soon learned all about it.

Kay explained that her mom was occasionally locked up in a ward of some type where she had to be constrained and watched constantly.

"What?" I exclaimed. "Really?"

Kay said that schizophrenia was a serious mental disorder that made her mom have hallucinations and delusions of crazy people talking to her and chasing her. Kay's mom was once seen running down their street in her pajamas, screaming, "Stay away from me! Don't hurt me! Someone please help me!" There was no one chasing her, and that's when some men in the white jackets came to lock her up again. When these professional types found out she was also a witch, things got even worse for Kay's mom. I don't think anyone understood the witch part of her personality, since they could barely handle her craziness.

Kay said the men took her mom to the county hospital where she was put in a special room for people with this mental illness. Her mom didn't like it there, so one day, when no one was watching, she tied all her bed sheets together and climbed out the window and escaped. She somehow returned home the next day—no one knows how since it's twenty-plus miles from the hospital to her home. According to Kay, that was the last time her mom was locked up anywhere, yet apparently, her episodes of going nuts continued.

Sometimes I wondered how Kay and her siblings coped with all this craziness. It never occurred to me that maybe they didn't or couldn't … that maybe, just maybe, they had the same problem, too.

Forever Friends ...
Gone Forever

During our senior year of high school, Kay started acting peculiar and saying outrageous things to me and our other friends. She would say things like "people were following me" or "people are watching me." I knew it wasn't true and tried to reassure her, but Kay kept on acting weird. Finally, Jean said to me, "Patty, I think Kay is losing her marbles. I'm going to stay away from her. All our other friends think she's just plain nuts, too."

I had to agree with them, but at the same time, I couldn't just reject Kay. She was losing friends left and right. I was the only one remaining who would still listen to her crazy stories of being followed, being paranoid, and even being pregnant. I knew there was no way she was pregnant. Kay had never had a boyfriend, and I knew for sure that she hadn't had sex yet. It was all in her head.

Things got worse for Kay. She became even more delusional, and with all these wild thoughts coming from her mind, she started acting downright insane. Soon all of her friends had deserted her, and she became a ward of the state of Minnesota. This meant she had to live in a designated apartment building that was monitored with cameras everywhere and guards positioned at each entrance and exit. It appeared that she was repeating her mom's history of craziness (yes, it did run in the family).

Kay was prescribed medicines to help stabilize her mental state, but sometimes she'd forget to take her pills. Sometimes when she had forgotten to take her medication, she'd call me and say things like, "Patty, I have a black boyfriend. He's here with me now, and I'm baking chocolate chip cookies for him. You'd like him. His name's Izzy. And, Patty, I'm having a baby in a month. Can you come and visit me when the baby comes? I'm going to name him Vincent as in the artist since I have a feeling it's a boy. I'll bake more cookies, and you can bring the coffee."

"Yes, Kay," I'd promise, "I'll come by one of these days with coffee. Good luck with your new boyfriend. I'll call you in a couple days."

After hearing similar stories about Kay's phone calls to other friends, I figured out that none of this was true. There was no Izzy, no baby, and probably no chocolate chip cookies, that's because she wasn't allowed an oven because she had a habit of hurting herself with it. Her stove didn't work either. I knew this from the last time I had visited her. Her life had become sad and lonely, and she was very much her own worst enemy. Her siblings never visited. I'm not sure why. Maybe they were embarrassed. Maybe they feared Kay was just like their mom. Although I believed this to be true, I remained her friend until the end, which came much too soon.

One late fall afternoon, just a year after graduation while I was attending business school in St. Paul, our phone rang. Mom answered, and someone at the other end of the line said he had some bad news for Patti. The man told Mom that no one had seen Kay for weeks. Then one day, one of the therapists who lived in the apartment building had walked past Kay's apartment door and smelled something horrible. The therapist got a master key and went inside to find, much to her horror, Kay dead, half-dangling off her torn and ragged couch. They said she must have been dead for two weeks from the way her body looked and smelled.

When I arrived home that evening, Mom had a look of shock on her face and said, "Patty, sit down, I have some very sad news to tell you."

"What Mom? What's wrong?" I asked.

Mom said, "Kay's dead. They found her body today in her apartment. Apparently, she had been dead for two weeks from what she looked like."

"Mom! Mom! No! No!" I cried. "This can't be. I was just there a month ago to visit, and she was doing so well … looked so happy. Who found her? Does her family know?"

Mom said, "Honey, I don't know. Maybe you can call one of her brothers or her older sister to find out more details."

"Oh, God," I said. "This is so horrible. Poor Kay."

Her funeral was the following week. The only ones present were her immediate family, me, and one other schoolmate who still cared enough to show up. No one else from our class came. I couldn't understand why.

How cold can people be? I wondered. Didn't they know this was not her fault and that she was seriously ill from a mental problem? Our schoolmates were not her friends. They had abandoned her years before.

I had promised Kay and Jean that we would remain best friends forever. Kay was gone now, but I still had Jean, or so I thought.

The Accident

Jean and I had been best friends since the seventh grade. We spent so much time together; some folks thought we were twins. There's no doubt I loved her like a sister, and I truly believed we would always be Best Friends Forever. However, even the closest siblings or friends part company eventually to pursue personal dreams and follow their own life's path. So it was with Jean and me.

Shortly after graduating from high school, Jean fell madly in love with a guy named Mike. I guess they would be called hippies now, because the two of them ran off to join the Flower Power movement in San Francisco. They took just a few belongings with them since they had decided to hitchhike from Minnesota to California so they could see the sights and stop to smell the roses along the way. This wasn't unusual. They were just being thrifty. All of us hitchhiked back then. In those days, it was a fun, cheap, and safe way to travel.

Jean and Mike eventually made it all the way to Northern California. They were hitchhiking through the redwood forests just north of Trinidad, California, where they figured, if they were lucky enough to catch a ride with someone heading south, they would be in San Francisco by nightfall. As luck would have it, a nice older couple spotted them and pulled over to offer them a lift. They said were heading to San Francisco, too, and would gladly take them all the way into the city. Jean and Mike climbed into the backseat happily anticipating their arrival at the city of their destiny, San Francisco.

About half way there, the car they were riding in got a flat. The driver carefully pulled to the side of the road and parked the car. Even though they were traveling on a very narrow, windy road, he probably had no choice but to pull over to the shoulder; otherwise, he would have had to drive on the rim of the wheel. The couple stopped the car and got out to change the tire, leaving Jean and Mike in the backseat. My guess is that they were probably asleep. At least, I pray they were.

As the older couple proceeded to switch out the tire, a massive logging truck hauling a full load of timber came barreling around a curve in the road. Evidently, the truck driver didn't see the car sitting half on, half off the shoulder in time and slammed into it . . killing Jean and Mike instantly. The force of the impact had thrown the elderly couple into the side ditch. They were found bruised but uninjured after the accident.

What happened next, no one really knows for sure. Perhaps this elderly couple flagged down the next car and were taken to a gas station or store with a phone booth. The only thing I know for sure is that the police came and so did an ambulance, although it took a while because the accident had happened deep in the redwood forest and a long way from Trinidad. Folks in White Bear never did get all the details. I had to piece the story together from newspaper and police reports to make sense of it.

Their bodies were shipped back to Minnesota, and an autopsy was performed. They found out that Jean was four months pregnant when she died, which made all this ten times worse for her parents and for me. Jean had always wanted to have a baby, but she never wanted to shame her parents like her sister Annie had. After losing Jean and her unborn child, the Olson's were never the same. Of course they weren't. Neither was I.

Strangely, to this day, when I am visiting my hometown of White Bear, some folks think they are seeing a ghost. For some reason, these locals never could tell us apart, so when they read about Jean's accident, they thought I had been killed. We looked that much alike. Sometimes people my age, old high school classmates, will stop me and say, "I thought you had died." That's when I say, "No, I'm Patty. It's Jean that is dead." It's heartbreaking, sad, and totally spooky when I have to clarify this matter to others. I quickly tell them the facts as I know them and move on. It's not a story I like to recall.

Losing my best friend as a teenager was devastating. Jean's death created a huge hole in my heart that remained an open wound for many years—making me wonder if I could ever have another friend as close as Jean and I were to each other. My twin was gone forever, but she still lived in my memories, where she

remains to this day. My very best friend forever, Jean, still lives—
forever young in mind and body—my soul sister … forever.

PART VI

FOR WHOM THE BELLS TOLLED (ALMOST)

Meeting Gene

With the exception of getting busted by the police for skinny-dipping, my friends and I managed to get through high school without encountering any crises or serious run-ins with the law, school officials, or our folks, which was amazing considering some of the wild and crazy pranks we pulled on a regular basis. We were a fun-loving, carefree bunch of daredevils, but for the most part, we managed to stay out of trouble, regardless of our numerous peccadilloes. By our senior year, however, the group had started to splinter. Kay had begun acting weird, and Jean had fallen in love with a handsome hippie. So by the time graduation rolled around, everyone seemed ready to follow their own paths and get on with their lives. Perhaps that mind-set partially explains what almost happened to me the summer of '70. That was the summer I met Gene from East St. Paul.

That summer, I spent almost every weekend at the Trio Inn in Centerville with my longtime girlfriend, Jody. Centerville was just a few miles north of White Bear, and the "inn" was really an out-of-the-way country saloon with great pool tables and Schlitz on tap. It's the place where Jody and I got pretty darn good at shooting pool and the place we often left with a quite a bit of extra cash from our winning bets. That made hanging out at the Trio fun and worthwhile!

One particular wonderfully warm Friday night, Jody and I were hanging out at the bar waiting for our turn on the best table, the one closest to the exit (the exit being the back door, just in case we needed to leave abruptly), and enjoying our favorite beer when I noticed a tall, dark, greaser-type guy, dressed all in black, walking in that same back door. The stranger standing in the doorway stared at us, giving us the once over. We'd been coming here since the snow thaw (at least six weeks), so we knew this was a new face in town. My first glance told me he had his eyes on Jody, not me, so I said,

"Who's that guy, Jody? Has he ever been in here when we were here? He's kind of interesting, don't you think?"

Jody replied, "Good God, Patty, he's a greaser. When did you start liking old guys with slicked-back hair?"

"Oh, shut up!" I snapped. "His eyes are piercing right through you. He's looking at you, Jody, not me."

"Bullshit!" Jody said. "He's definitely not my type."

"What do you mean, 'not your type'? Hell, he kind of looks like your brother Gimp with all that black greasy hair."

At that remark, Jody nudged me in the ribs and said, "Fuck off. No way," and we both started laughing.

Meanwhile, Mr. Greaser Man made his way to the bar. "Hi, Gene. Long time, no see. Where ya been, man?" asked Carl, the bartender.

"I've been out to sea for a few months. I just got home on leave. I have four weeks to spend with my family, ride my Harley, hang out here, and enjoy the company of some fine-looking women like these two here," he said, turning to me and Jody and flashing a huge grin that showed off his very large, very even, pearly white teeth. Up close, he was actually rather handsome.

He was too old for me. I knew that for sure, but still, he was handsome in a different kind of way. It might have been his large blue-green eyes that got my attention. Before any of us could say anything else, I noticed our table was empty. "Looks like our table's open," I said, "Let's play. Maybe this guy will get a kick out of what sharp-shooters we are."

"Ha!" Jody replied.

Taking our places at our pool table (we liked to think it was ours and ours alone since it was the best one in the bar), Jody opened with a nice clean break, dropping three balls into the pockets. The new face in town smirked and approached the table slowly, walking from end to end. Although that kind of made me anxious, I played one of my best games ever. Finally, he said, "Hi, my name is Gene. How about I take the two of you on?" He proceeded to lay a five on the table as I said, "Hi, I'm Patty, and this is my girlfriend Jody. Sure, let's play." I was always open to new experiences. Jody was too.

The first two games, he slaughtered us. The third game was ours and so was the fourth, making us even-steven. I pulled Jody to the side, away from this new guy named Gene, and said, "Let's show this guy what we've got," and we proceeded to do just that for the tiebreaker. We beat his butt good!

"Good game, girls," he said, handing me the five. "Want a beer and some popcorn?"

"Sure," we both said as we sat down, one on each side of our new pool-playing friend.

With beers in hand, we chatted up a storm. "Do you live around here? Are you in the Navy? Do you come here a lot?" Jody asked.

Gene didn't seem to mind all the questions. "Yes, I come here whenever I'm home. This is my favorite country bar. It's great riding on these long rural roads, nice and peaceful. I like getting away from the freeways and the city."

I said, "So you're just home for four weeks? Too bad you can't take the whole summer off and then go back."

Gene smiled good-naturedly. "Sugar, that's not how it works. I would never do anything to upset the Navy folks. I love serving my country." That's noble, I thought. This Mr. Greaser Man dressed all in black was actually a nice guy. Looks can be deceiving.

It was getting late when Jody turned to me and said, "Patty, we better head home, I have to babysit my sister's two brats all weekend. She's leaving early in the morning for our cabin near Spooner to spend a couple of days with her new lover boy."

"Okay." I replied. As I got up off the bar stool, Gene gently tapped my arm. "Are you dating anybody?" he asked. "Can I call you?"

In utter amazement I said, "Um, sure, have a pen?" I gave him my phone number and said, "Nice meeting you, Gene. We've got to go home now, but yeah, call me. I'd love to ride that Harley of yours. I ride my brothers' bikes whenever I can."

The next day, midday, the phone rang. Mom answered, and then cupping the receiver said, "Patty, it's some guy named Gene. Who is he?"

I whispered, "Mom, keep it down. It's a guy I met last night when I was out with Jody."

"Alright, alright, tell me about it later," she said handing me the receiver.

"Hi, how are you today?" I said, stretching the curlicues out of the telephone cord.

"Fine," he answered. "How are you doing?"

"Great. It's a beautiful day," I chirped, hoping he'd make good on his promise to give me a ride on his Harley.

"It sure is," Gene said, "so how about I come and pick you up on my bike, and we can ride around the lake or go over to Stillwater?"

"Hold on a second," I said, "let me ask my mom."

I turned to Mom who was standing nearby and listening to my side of the conversation. "Mom, Gene wants to take me on a motorcycle ride. Is that okay with you?"

"Sure, honey, but tell him I want to meet this new guy named Gene."

I nodded, "Yes, Mom," turning my attention back to Gene. "Sure, what time?"

"I can leave my house in about a half hour," he said, "and it'll take me about a half hour to get to White Bear. Does that give you enough time to get ready?"

"Sure," I said, and then gave him our address and the directions.

"Be sure to wear jeans as the pipes can get hot on your legs," he said before hanging up. How exciting to be going on my first motorcycle ride of the season—and on a Harley to boot! How fun!

I hurriedly dressed in my newest pair of blue jeans and a bright, floral blouse and then tied my waist-long hair into a ponytail and put on my tennis shoes. As I came into the kitchen to wait for Gene to arrive, Mom said, "Who the hell is this guy, Patty? Did you meet him at the pool hall?"

"Yes, Mom, I met him with Jody last night. He came in, and we played a few games of pool. Afterwards he bought us a drink. He's a little older, but he's a real sweet guy—he even has good manners. I think you'll like him, Mom."

"I hope so," she replied with a hint of optimism.

From the time I graduated, I could sense that Mom was ready to get me married off. I think it was called "old school" thinking. Anyway, I'm sure she figured that marriage was the safest and surest way to get me out of her house and out of her hair. I knew she was interested in this new guy, Gene, but I wanted to say, "Don't hold your breath, Mom. There's no way I'm gonna marry Mr. Greaser Man. First, he's way too old, and second, he has way too much slicked-back black hair for my taste," or so I thought. He arrived forty minutes later, and as he was parking his very loud and beautiful Harley in our driveway, Mom peered out the front window and said, "Dear God, he looks like one of the singers from Sha-Na-Na. Where in the hell did you find this guy?"

I said, "Mom, calm down. He's walking up the sidewalk. He probably heard you." To which she replied, "I don't give a shit; I want to meet this Gene guy."

Before he had a chance to knock, I answered the door and said, "Hi Gene, you got here quickly. I'm glad you figured out my directions."

"No problem," he said. "White Bear is easy to get around in."

At that point, Mom came out of the kitchen, where she must have put on a little lipstick. Smiling her best Mom smile, she said, "Hi, I'm Mom. Patty tells me you are in the Navy. How long are you on leave?"

Gene answered her in a most gentlemanly way. "Yes, ma'am; nice to meet you. I'm home for four weeks. After meeting your lovely daughter last night, I have a feeling this may be the best four weeks of my life. That is, if she agrees."

Mom seemed to relax before my eyes, and then she replied with a taste of honey on her tongue, "You kids go and have fun, but have her home by dark. I don't mind her riding on the back of a bike when it's light out, but I don't trust those damn bikes at night."

"Yes, ma'am, she'll be home before dark." Gene promised.

"Bye, Mom, and thanks," I said as Gene and I left for the first of many motorcycle rides we'd enjoy during the next few weeks. I was ready for the time of my life with this new guy. Who knew what might happen? Plus, I knew Mom was quite impressed by his good manners, calling her ma'am, and all.

Gene made sure I was seated securely before taking off and turning onto Highway 6. He headed north, and we sped along all the way to Hugo. With the wind blowing in our hair, I was overcome with a feeling of complete freedom and joy. I was having the time of my life. When we arrived in Hugo, Gene turned his head and asked if I wanted to stop at the A&W for a root beer. "Of course," I said, "I love their root beer, Let's do it."

Pulling into the A&W, Gene parked the Harley and ordered two large drinks. As we stretched our legs and sipped our sodas, Gene looked over at me and asked, "Are you sure you don't have a steady? You're a beautiful girl; you must have someone special in your life."

"Not right now," I said with a definite sense of relief. "I just broke up with a jerk named Jeff. It ended a month ago. I've been hanging out with Jody, D, and my other girlfriends for the past few weeks, swimming, messing around, and just having fun. Can I ask you a question?"

"Of course, shoot," he replied.

"How old are you?" I asked.

"I'm twenty-eight. Is that too old for you? I hope not."

"Nope, I'm seventeen. That's just eleven years' difference. Not a problem, as far as I'm concerned." The truth was, I really didn't see the age difference as any problem. He apparently was young inside—maybe as young as I was inside—and to my way of thinking, that's all that mattered.

By now, it was mid-afternoon. We continued riding, this time heading toward the St. Croix River and Stillwater. Coming down the big hill approaching the river, the sky looked bluer than I had ever remembered, and the river appeared polka-dotted with speedboats, pontoons, and all sizes of yachts. It was the perfect day to be on the river, or better yet, on the back of a Harley. As we rode on, I wrapped my arms around Gene's waist. I could tell that he was in great shape because his stomach was tight and strong. I guessed that Navy men must really have to stay in good shape if they were going to serve our country. I liked that. No doubt, he was looking better to me. Even his hair looked like it had less crap in it. It was flying all over the place, as was mine. I loved that free look and secretly thought to myself that if this relationship went anywhere, I could easily get him to wear his hair in a more hip fashion. I was sure of it. Without all that greasy hair stuff, I saw hope not only for his hair, but maybe even more.

We rode through town and then took the historic Stillwater Bridge across the river to Wisconsin. Crossing the bridge, we were treated to a bird's-eye view of all the boats sailing up and down the St. Croix on this glorious summer day. We spent the next hour riding along the banks of the river, just enjoying the day, before turning back toward Hudson, where we stopped for a late lunch. We got a table at a little riverside café and sat as close as possible to the beach. Gene ordered beers and hamburgers with fries for the two of us and then looked at me and said, "Are you having fun, Gorgeous?"

I could hardly contain my enthusiasm. "Oh my God, it is such beautiful day! I'm having a great time, and I love riding on the back of your bike. It's just perfect. Thanks for lunch, too."

Gene gazed into my eyes and said, "How about we do this again tomorrow? I only have one month's leave before I go back to Midway Island."

"Wow!" I replied, "So soon? Why does the Navy just give you a month at home?"

"That's just the way it is," he said. "Are you game for tomorrow? If it's another nice day, we could ride to Afton and have lunch at the Afton Inn. Sound good to you?"

"Yeah, if Mom allows it, I'm game."

We finished our lunch, got back on the Harley, and this time took the Hudson Bridge to the Minnesota side of the river heading back toward White Bear. It had been an absolutely perfect day, which doesn't come that often given Minnesota's summer storms and bad weather. Pulling up in the front of my house right at sunset, Gene parked the Harley and walked me to the door. "Can I pick you up, say around eleven tomorrow morning? Do you get up early?"

"Yes, I'm always up early." I said, trying not to sound too eager. "I'll be ready by eleven."

"Great," Gene said climbing back on his Harley. "I'll see you tomorrow, then," he said and waved good night. As promised, he had me home before dark. I knew that would make Mom happy, and I was happy too. In fact, I was beaming with delight after spending the most wonderful day of my life with my new friend, Gene.

My Second Date with Gene

The next morning, as Mom and I sat at the kitchen table and sipped a second cup of coffee, I heard the rumble of Gene's bike coming down Floral Drive. Mom heard it too and said, "Honey, he seems like a really nice guy. Do you like him?"

"Yes, Mom, I do. He's a really nice guy, and I absolutely love his motorcycle. Plus, he's a safe driver and doesn't show off on the road or speed. You should be happy about that."

"I am, dear. I know bikes can be a lot of fun, but just make sure you hang on tight. You never know when the road ahead will take an unexpected twist or turn."

Just then, Gene rang the doorbell and Mom answered with a bright smile. "Good morning. It looks like another beautiful day to be out riding bikes. You two go and have fun, but how about being back here by six? If you want, Gene, you can join us for supper. I'm making a pot roast, plus brownies for dessert."

I said, "We'll be back by six, Mom, but Gene might need to get back to his own family for supper."

"No, no, I would love to join you for supper and meet your brothers and stepdad." Then turning his full attention on Mom, he flashed his most handsome smile and said, "I'll be sure to have us home by six."

Oh God, I thought, this is really moving too fast for me. I whispered to Mom as we walked out the door, "We'll see, Mom, we'll see."

Gene revved the bike's engine in the driveway while I climbed up and casually leaned in against him. "Your mom is so cool," he said waiting for me to get settled before taking off.

"Yes, she's cool and pushy, too. You don't have to meet my family if you don't want to," I said.

"Let's just see how the day goes," he said over the noise of the engine. "For now, let's just ride."

Pulling onto the highway, Gene headed the massive Harley toward Afton, about a forty-minute ride away. Northern Minnesotans are rarely treated to two gorgeous summer days in a row, but this morning was even more beautiful than the previous afternoon. Is this a sign? I wondered as we cruised down Afton's main street. Why, even the breeze is uplifting, I thought, noticing that the city park was full of kids casting colorful kites high into the sky. Could it get any better than this? I couldn't wait to find out.

Gene maneuvered the Harley into a parking space at the Afton Inn, one of the better restaurants in the area noted for their daily specials. The special this day happened to be a fresh catch of walleye served with wild rice and a salad of spring greens. We downed the meal with gusto and then topped it off with lemon meringue pie and hot coffee. As we waited for the check, Gene leaned back in his chair and patted his stomach with genuine satisfaction. "Another delicious meal with a beautiful girl ... what could be more perfect?"

"It was the best," I said. "They must have caught that fish first thing this morning—it was so fresh, and that pie tasted like it had come right out of the oven. Thanks, Gene."

Gene looked at me as I downed the last drops of coffee. His expression had changed, grown more serious, more intent. Finally, he said, "How about we get a bottle of wine and find a remote spot along the river?"

"Hmm, do you know a place somewhere away from all the homes and hidden from all the boats going by where we could skinny-dip?" I asked.

His face flushed, but his eyes flashed with sparks of anticipation. "There has to be an empty beach—probably if we head a little more south. Let's ride and find out." I was open to that suggestion. I always did love an adventure, and swimming naked, even with people I had just met, was one of my favorite pastimes.

We hopped back on the bike and this time rode south, stopping first at the corner liquor store to buy a bottle of Chianti before investigating all the dirt roads that led to the riverbanks. After twenty minutes or so, we saw an opening in the trees shading a narrow path. Gene stopped the bike, and I jumped off. Dashing down the path, I called back to him, "This way, Gene. Looks as if we've found our own private beach." Catching up to me, he took off his leather jacket and spread it like blanket for us to sit on. We were so nestled away, I was certain no one could see us—not even the boats that were far off in the distance.

"Turn around," I said, "don't look! I'm going to take a skinny-dip." Taking off my shoes, jeans, and top, I dove in and heard Gene holler, "Okay, it's your turn not to look. Dive under while I strip!" I did just that, and then he dove in and swam toward me, gently nudging my thigh as his head came up.

"Don't you love the free feeling of swimming in the raw?" I said. "Who needs a bathing suit? They just get in the way," I said as he shook his hair out of his eyes. Laughing, splashing, and swimming with and against the current, we flirted with each other, getting intimate, little by little. At last I said, "Turn away, Gene. I'm going on shore to soak up some sun." I guessed that he had not turned away but rather had followed my every move with his hungry eyes as I swam back to our cozy beach. I walked on shore and found a place to sunbathe, placing my jeans over my private parts, then giggled to myself as Gene said, "Don't look, I'm getting out too."

"I won't look. I promise," I said, as I watched him walk out of the water, before quickly looking away when he caught my gaze.

Grabbing his shirt to cover himself, he walked toward me and sat down on the leather jacket that was our blanket. He opened the wine, and we each took a sip as he commented on another glorious day adding, "You are a charming, fun, and adventurous young lady. I think I'm falling for you." Hearing that comment, my eyes got wider. I sensed what was happening between us, but all I said was, "I love having a good time, and you seem to be a pretty spontaneous and open guy, too."

"Yes, I'm definitely open to having fun," he said, and then we lay back and stretched out in afternoon sun, sipping the wine and enjoying this magical moment in time. At some point, I must have fallen asleep because I was awakened by Gene kissing me. Startled, I sat up and said playfully, "What are you doing?"

"Kissing you, my sweet girl. I couldn't resist. Should I stop?" I shook my head softly from side to side. "No, don't stop." We continued kissing, and as he embraced me, we rolled together in the sand, gently touching each other's bodies for the first time.

"You are the most beautiful thing I have ever seen," Gene said, and I replied, "I bet you say that to all your girlfriends."

"I haven't had a girlfriend in a couple years. The Navy has kept me busy at sea for a long, long time.

"How long?" I asked.

"I've been on that ship, for the last three years, unable to establish any kind of a lasting relationship. Most girls don't want a guy who is gone all the time. Plus, I have to head back soon. This time I'll be stationed on Midway Island, which is a hell of a faraway place."

"Where is it, Midway Island?" I asked.

"Way out there, somewhere in the middle of the Pacific Ocean. That's why they call it Midway," he said.

"Oh my, that is far away," I said trying to fix a place in my mind but realizing that afternoon shadows had begun to darken the corners of our secret beach. "Yikes! Do you have the time? We'd better head back, so we can be home in time for dinner. We may need a little time to clean up, too. If we walk in with all this sand on our clothes, Mom will really wonder what we've been up to," I said, knowing there would be hell to pay if we were late.

"Maybe I better not come for supper tonight, Patty," Gene said. "Maybe next week or next weekend will work better. We are both kind of a mess, and I want to make a good first impression with your stepdad and brothers."

"Whatever you're comfortable with doing. My brother Melvin will definitely like you and your Harley. Johnny will simply be curious."

It was ten minutes to six when Gene parked the Harley in front of our house. "How about I meet your family next week?" Gene said. "I feel as if I need a shower, and I don't want to make a bad first impression."

"Okay with me," I replied. "Thanks for another fabulous day." To this, he smiled and gave me a sweet kiss on the lips—my goodness! I had never yet been kissed like that. It was a Wow! No, it was more like a big WOW! This relationship was moving right along. I had met a nice, trustworthy, mature guy. All was right with the world. Our age difference didn't matter one bit, I told myself as I floated through the front door.

The Announcement

The following weekend, Gene called and asked if I wanted to go for a ride since it was another beautiful summer morning. "I have just two weeks left," he said, "and I want to spend as much of that time with you as I can."

How sweet, I thought, as I hung up the phone after agreeing that he could pick me up in an hour, right before lunch.

Mom, who apparently was listening to our conversation, said, "Honey, you have met a nice guy. I hope you appreciate him. As you know from my experience, good men are hard to find."

"Yes, Mom, he is nice. He treats me really good and is a lot of fun too." From Mom's look, it was obvious that she was hoping this was *the one* for me. In fact, I wondered if she wasn't almost hoping we'd run off together and elope.

I was sitting on our front patio when I recognized the rumbling noise of Gene's Harley—the echo could be heard for blocks around. Gene pulled into our driveway wearing a beautiful light blue jacket that complemented his eyes and the biggest smile I had ever seen on his face. Gosh, he's really happy to see me, I thought, feeling good about him and about us. Just as I was about to jump on the back of the bike, Mom yelled from inside the front screen door, "You kids have fun now."

"Yes, Mom," we both chimed simultaneously. Yep, no doubt about it, Mom was ready to set me free.

This day we rode to Como Park, the huge, lush park next to beautiful Como Lake outside St. Paul. We parked the bike and went into the park office where we rented a cute little maroon paddleboat. The temperature was ideal, around eighty degrees, and the sky a cloudless, brilliant blue. It was a perfect day to paddle about on the calm water and look at all the lovely waterfront homes. I was thinking we should rent a couple of trail bikes next and take the bike path around the lake when Gene turned toward me and said, "Patty, I know we have only dated a couple times, but I feel that I have fallen head over heels in love with you."

I must have jumped off my seat a foot or two at that statement because the boat tipped suddenly in my direction. "Gene, you are a lot of fun and a sweet man. I am having the time of my life with you, but are you sure you're already in love with me? I mean *really* sure?" I asked.

"I'm sure …," Gene replied, *"really sure!"*

"But you're leaving in a couple weeks. I don't want to fall in love if you have to leave for a year or two. How could I live like that?"

"You can come with me."

"What? How can I come with you? You're being sent to Midway Island, which is halfway around the world from here. How can I come with you?"

Sensing I was feeling pretty rattled by his unexpected declarations and ideas, he got really quiet for a few minutes, as if he wanted to think through what he wanted to say next. Then, he dropped the bomb. "Patty, will you marry me?"

This time, I nearly did fall overboard. My feet fell off the pedals, and my hands fell to my stomach. Clutching my wrenching gut, I said, "What? Married? I'm only seventeen. I'm too young to marry." I felt as if I had had the wind knocked out of me; however, as I tried to catch my breath and regain my composure, Gene calmly continued, "We could get married in your church. I'm sure my family won't mind. They're not that religious and would rather see me married than worry about what the Catholic Church thought."

By now, I felt entirely overwhelmed. "Let's go have lunch so I can think better," I suggested. "Food always helps me to think more clearly." Not only was that the truth, it was also the best answer I could come up with at the time.

"How about The Lexington on Grand? It can be our official engagement lunch," he said, smiling as if he had just landed a prize catch.

"Please, please. Let's just go now," I said, still feeling a bit queasy about this sudden turn of events.

We got back on the bike and rode to The Lexington in St. Paul, which just so happened to be my favorite restaurant in the Twin Cities. I was *so* ready for a good meal. I think Gene was quickly figuring out how much I loved to eat and that good food could make my brain work so much better. As soon as we arrived, he got a quiet table near the back, and I went to the ladies' room to freshen up. I needed a few minutes alone, not only to brush my hair and straighten up my appearance but more so to straighten out my rushing, rambling thoughts. I was in shock.

As I made my way to the intimate, corner table Gene had chosen for us, I saw him watching me with the most loving look on his face imaginable. I need food, I thought as I sat down, acting more shy than usual. He noticed my timidity and said, "Did I scare you? Are you in shock? Can you believe that I have fallen in love with you in the short time since we met? No matter if you believe me or not, I have. I've fallen hard, and I have a feeling you may be falling in love with me, too. I don't want to live without you, Patty. I want to take you with me. It would be the greatest adventure of your life."

Still in shock, I looked at him and said, "Let's order. I'm starving. They have the best steaks around, and I'm hungry for a rib eye or maybe their sirloin. How about you?"

Realizing I was avoiding the subject, Gene dropped it for the time being. "I could go for a nice, juicy steak, too, especially since you say they have the best in St. Paul," he said, motioning for the waiter to come and take our order. We each selected the rib eye with a baked potato, side salad, and iced teas to drink.

While we waited for our meal, I finally asked, "What is Midway Island like? What is there to do there? Do other sailors have wives there too? Is there a nice beach? Do they have good waves? Maybe I could learn to surf." Evidently, Gene enjoyed being bombarded by all my questions because he leaned forward and smiled, "Yes, there is all that and a bowling alley too."

"Oh boy, a bowling alley? I'll take the beach instead." (Of course, I knew how to bowl ... nearly everyone in Minnesota does, partly to survive the long, cold winters.) Gene said, "So, is this a maybe?"

"Feed me first, and I'll let you know. My brain is tired from thinking about so much so fast."

The meal was divine, and as I ate, my body and mind started to relax, although I was still pondering the idea of being married, leaving White Bear Lake for a huge adventure, and going out into the wide world as a married lady. The idea, although confusing, made some sense to me. Nothing much was happening in my life before I met Gene. Life had become kind of boring. In some ways, I was ready to get on with a new one. I just wasn't sure I was ready yet for this new life. One thing I was sure about, however, is that Mom would jump for joy at this announcement.

Gene paid the check and put his arm around me as we walked out and got back onto the Harley. With a slight breeze blowing across our faces and in our hair, we turned back toward White Bear. Back in our driveway, I said, "Gene, I need time to think. How about we take a break from each other for a little while?" Gene said, "Honey, whatever you need."

I hopped off the bike and went into the house, feeling dazed. It was a good thing no one was there to greet me because I went to my room and sank into my bed. Sleep came quickly. My confused mind needed to be less confused. Later that afternoon, Mom came into my room and said, "Sweetie, are you alright? Why are you sleeping in the middle of the day?"

"Mom, make some coffee. We need to talk," I said, with a noticeable tone of weariness and worry.

She looked at me with a mixture of genuine concern. "What's wrong, dear? Did Gene do something to hurt you? Are you okay?"

"Yes, Mom, I'm okay. Call me when the coffee's ready, and we'll talk. Johnny's not home is he?"

"No, he went off with Toad to a movie." Great. We had the house to ourselves. I could unload my thoughts on Mom. Although I knew that she was good and ready to get me married off, I was hoping she could help me sort out my feelings about this life-changing decision. To her, marriage would be the right thing to do. She'd probably say that I would love him soon enough and that good men are hard to find ... blah, blah, blah. I closed my eyes again and stayed in bed until I smelled the coffee.

Stumbling into the kitchen, I plopped down at the table and cupped the coffee mug in both hands. "Oh, Mom, what a day I've had," I said.

"You look tired and fragile. What the hell's going on?"

"You're never going to believe this, but Gene asked to marry me! We have only had a few dates, and I like him and all that, but come on. It's way too soon to ask this, don't you think?"

Mom's eyes were nearly popping out of her head. Then, with a sly grin she said, "My goodness, that Gene! He does work fast. You've got to hand it to him, he only had a few weeks to find a bride, and it looks like he has! Honey, this is wonderful news. You can lead that life of wild abandonment you've always wanted, travel the world, and get out of White Bear Lake once and for all. You know what I think of most of the local boys; they'll never amount to anything, more than likely end up working at the car lots or in some shitty garage fixing flat tires and renting snow blowers. Gene is a Navy man. He has a future. Think serious about this, honey."

I knew this would be her opinion. Looking at Gene, she probably saw him as God's answer to her prayers. Brother! Now what do I do? With an even more exhausted tone than before, I said, "Please Mom, keep this to yourself. I need to lie down and rest. I don't want to think about any of this. If Gene calls, tell him I'm too tired to see him right now. Please, Mom."

"Yes, dear, you rest. It'll all make sense to you tomorrow. Are you hungry? Have you eaten anything?" Even Mom knew a full stomach always helped me think better.

"No, thanks, I had a big lunch with Gene. I'm not hungry now," I said, yawning. Sleep came easily after my conversation with Mom, and as I drifted off, I dreamt of swimming and surfing off the coast of Midway Island and enjoying a wonderful, exciting life away from small town nothingness. Maybe Mom was right. Maybe this was the best way out after all. I slept the rest of that day. I must have been exhausted, or then again, it could have been I just wanted to spend the rest of my life in a dream world.

The Proposal

On a Saturday evening late in the season, I finally said yes to Gene's proposal. Thinking it would be fun to return to the place where we met, I suggested we drive out to the Trio Inn where we could play some pool and decide … as in decide if we were ready to be married.

The Trio's resident drunk, Damn Dennis, was in his regular place at the bar when we walked in. I don't know why everyone called him Damn Dennis. He was generally a friendly old coot who came in every night, sat on the same exact barstool as if it had his name engraved on it, and proceeded to drink his weight in draft beer until closing. He also greeted everyone who came in the tavern just as if he owned the place. Spotting us as we came through the same back door Gene had used the night we met, Dennis hollered out, "Hey guys, where ya been? Long time no see. What, are you two a couple now?"

I grinned sheepishly and felt my cheeks flush as Gene hollered back, "I have met the love of my life. This doll is my baby now." When I heard that comment, I thought I should feel complimented, but I was half wondering whether I could get used to being called his baby, his doll, his wife. Could I? I wasn't sure. Something nagged at my conscience.

While waiting for a table to open, we sat at the bar, ordered a couple beers, and munched on some popcorn and a bowl of peanuts. As we chatted with Dennis and Carl, the bartender, the back door swung open again. This time, in walked D and Jody. They quickly made their way toward us. Knowing that Gene and I had been hanging out together ever since we'd met here a month ago, D greeted us with a huge smile. "What a cute couple you two make!" she said. "Where ya been, Patty? I've tried calling you several times, but your mom always says that you are out with

Gene. Sounds like you've been having the time of your life with this guy."

"Yeah, we've been all over on Gene's motorcycle ... out to lunch, riding along the river ... just having a great time. What have you been up to?" I asked, hoping to change the subject.

"Swimming a lot at the county beach and babysitting my sister's kids. I met this guy named Pete; we've been dating and having fun. He kind of looks like B. J. Thomas, you know, that singer who sings "Raindrops Keep Falling on My Head.""

"Super," I said. "I'm glad for you. B. J. Thomas is kind of cute."

A table opened up, so Gene left us while he set up the balls and chalked a couple of the straightest sticks. Handing me the shorter one, he said, "Ok, honey, let's play." D and Jody heard his comment and looked at me in a sly, playful way that suggested they could see that our relationship was moving right along.

We played and drank for two more hours before Gene whispered in my ear, "Hey gorgeous, how about we find a nice spot to go skinny-dipping in White Bear Lake?"

I nodded in agreement and whispered back, "Yes, yes, let's get out of this place. I could go for a moonlight swim." As we said our goodbyes to Jody, D and the rest of the locals hanging at the bar, all heads turned to watch us leave. They all seemed to have that knowing look of mischief in their eyes. Finally, Damn Dennis said, "Have fun kids."

"Absolutely," I yelled, not looking back.

This night, we drove to the Mahtomedi side of the lake, making our way toward the peninsula. Gene spotted a dirt road that looked dark and barren, so he pulled the bike off onto the beach and parked it behind a large group of trees. We were very much alone—just how we wanted to be—hidden from a world of prying eyes. A full moon scattered glimmering, flickering lights across the lake's surface, making the bouncing moonbeams look like iridescent dragonflies dancing on the water. It was magical. We both stripped as I said, "Last one in is a rotten egg." Laughing, we dove into the water, feeling the freedom of being naked in the moonlight. We caressed and kissed as Gene said, "Marry me. I love you." Caught up in the beauty and wonder of the moment, I said, "Yes, Gene. I'll marry you." After that, I experienced the most passionate two hours of my young life.

We made love in the water, and on the beach, and it was a genuinely tender, glorious experience for both of us. At one point, Gene said, "I wonder if we can plan a wedding in a week? Can you talk to your minister at the Lutheran Church? Aren't Lutherans fairly easy to talk to? You know him well, right?"

"Boy, I have no idea," I said, my mind swirling around this new idea like ripples on the lake, "but I'm sure Mom can help. Pastor Sorenson is a nice guy. But, how will we tell all our family and all my schoolmates?" I asked.

"Oh, don't worry about that. I'm certain things will work out just fine. Still, I better get you home now before your mom kicks my ass."

"You got that right!" I said. "Once I'm married, though, she won't be able to boss us around anymore. That'll be nice."

"Yes, it will!" Gene said, giving me one last emphatic kiss as he lifted me onto the Harley.

Thankfully, everyone was asleep when I got home. I crept down the stairs to my basement bedroom and crashed, stretching my tingling body across the bed. Not only was I feeling loved, I was feeling wide open, free, and exhausted. Now, in the dark comfort of my bedroom, I crawled in between the cool sheets, curled up, closed my eyes, and fell into a deep, peaceful sleep.

Run, Baby, Run

Mom wasn't surprised or upset by my decision to marry Gene. In fact, I think she was happy to get me married off so quickly. However, she was a bit surprised and upset when I told her we only had ten days to plan my wedding. She stewed about it all day Sunday and then woke me early the next morning, yelling down the basement stairs, "Better get up and get going, Patty. We don't have much time to get you a wedding dress and shoes. I thought we'd head over to St. Paul this morning. There's a nice bridal store near Como Avenue. Let's just hope they have some size eight dresses on the rack because there's no time to order anything."

"I'll be ready in a flash, Mom." I said, heaving a sigh of relief as I jumped out of bed and pulled on my blue jeans. Thank goodness! Mom had evidently made up her mind to take charge. I knew for certain that if anyone could pull off a major event like a wedding in ten days, Mom could; so if she said, "Get up and get going," I wasn't about to keep her waiting.

This is going to be so exciting, I thought, as Mom drove us into the city, but when we walked into the bridal shop, my enthusiasm took a nosedive. "Oh, Mom," I gasped, "these look like old-lady wedding dresses. I sure hope they have something for a teenager." Just then, a saleslady approached us. "Welcome to the Como Park Bridal Store. My name is Sissy. How can I assist you today?"

Mom said, "This young lady needs a sweet, simple, and affordable wedding gown that can be fitted within a week. Her wedding is at the end of the month."

Sissy smiled and nodded reassuringly. "No problem. We have a few cute dresses in the back just right for this young lady. You're about a size ten, right?"

"No, I'm a size eight," I hissed. "I just look like a ten because I'm big boned." As I said this, Mom gave me the funniest look ever, but Sissy just smirked, leaving us on our own while she went to the back room to look for my perfect wedding dress. Mom and I sat down on a pair of plush, pink-flowered chairs to wait, and within minutes, Sissy returned with two dresses for me to choose from.

The first one was a fluffy, overdone foo-foo number with way too much lace. I took one look at it and said, "No, no, no! I hate lace. It makes me itch all over. I hope the next one's better." Sissy pulled the plastic from the second gown, and much to my amazement, I looked over at Mom and said, "That's kind of nice. What do you think?" Mom said, "Looks to me like it will do just fine. Try it on, honey."

Sissy placed the dress on the dressing room hook, and I went in to try it on, appearing moments later wearing my "just fine" wedding gown. It fit me to a T and was the right length too. I stood on the mirrored platform so I could view all sides of the dress—my wedding dress—the one I'd be wearing when I walked down the aisle in less than ten days. Mom's right, I thought, this will do just fine. So I said, "Okay Mom, you better ask the price now before I change my mind." And so Mom did, and we did—buy it, that is—and then we darted off to the shoe store in Maplewood to find a pair of "just fine" shoes to match my "just fine" dress.

That task being easily accomplished, the next thing we needed to do was order the wedding flowers. Fortunately, there was a fabulous floral shop on County Road E in White Bear that was noted for its beautiful and inexpensive arrangements. I chose an assortment of daisy-type flowers, mostly yellow and black, along with some orange petunias for my bouquet, while Mom selected a couple of flowery plants for the altar that could be replanted at home after the ceremony. (Remember, two for one? Mom always liked to get double value for her dollars.) By noon, we had completed all of the tasks on Mom's to-do list, so we treated ourselves to a quick lunch at the nearby Pizza Hut.

No doubt, things were coming together nicely for my big day. Now all I needed to do was tell D and all my friends that I was about to tie the knot, and that they all better show up to support me before I took off for Midway Island with my new husband, Gene. That didn't take long, either, because Jody's big mouth and her many siblings had told everyone in town about this crazy idea of Patty O marrying a sailor home on leave from the Navy, a guy she'd met not even a month ago at the Trio Inn. All our classmates asked who he was, and Jody later told me that she had told them that he was a much older, greaser-type guy with green eyes, black-slicked back hair, and a Harley that stole my heart. I don't think she actually believed all this, but that's what she said to convince all our friends to head down to the Lutheran Church on Highway 61 the last Saturday of the month.

As far as Mom was concerned, we were now ready for the big event. Having made all the arrangements for the ceremony, she was content that everything would run smoothly and the wedding would come off without a hitch. As for me, my adrenalin was flowing. I could visualize all the amazing adventures soon to come as I left my hometown of White Bear and headed off to an exotic tropical isle somewhere in the wild blue yonder. It was an exciting thought, but I was feeling drained. I figured all I needed to feel revved up again was a few days of complete rest, a bit of time alone to reflect upon my upcoming wedding and this life-changing decision. So, I did just that. I fell asleep and slept for three days straight.

"Gene's on the phone," Mom said, gently shaking me awake. It was now just two days before our wedding. He asked if I was okay and if he or his family needed to do anything to help. I asked Mom, and she said, "Tell him no. Everything's ready for your big day." So, I did just that. Then I hung up the phone and went back to sleep. I slept until Friday, the day before our wedding. When I woke up that morning, I had a sense of total enlightenment.

Standing before my small, round bedroom mirror, I looked deep into myself (probably for the very first time ever). "Oh shit," I said to the reflection in the mirror, "I can't do this. I can't run away and live on Midway Island. Even though Gene is a really nice guy ... and perhaps I really do love him ... after all, he has shown me a great time this summer ... and he's kind of cute, under that greasy hair ... and I really like his Harley ... and all that riding has been the best time ever ... and he's going to hate me when he finds out ... I am not going through with this!" I ran up the stairs and down the hall, grabbed my mom by her cute little hand, and said, "Quick, come to my bedroom. Now—please! It's important, very important."

As I shut my bedroom door, I asked Mom to come sit on my bed with me. "Honey, what's wrong?" she asked. "What's the matter?" I started crying. "Mom, I can't do this. I've had time to think things through, and I just cannot marry Gene. I'd be running away from my life here to a strange place with a strange man for a strange life. It's not that I don't love adventure; it just doesn't feel right to me. I'm not sure if I really love him." (I said through tons of tears.) "I like him a whole lot, that's for sure. But I don't think I know what true love feels like. I'm just not sure. Mom! What am I going to do?" I asked, by this time balling my eyes out and sobbing beyond belief … bewildered and confused.

Mom rocked me in her arms and said, "Sweetheart, if it doesn't feel right, it is probably not right. If there's one thing I've learned through all my bad times, is that if it doesn't feel right, don't do it. I don't want you to worry now. I'll handle all this. You just lie low for a few days. Don't answer the door or the phone. I'll take care of everything." With a quick and tearful reply, I said, "And please tell Gene that I care for him deeply. I'm just uncertain and confused, please Mom?" Mom reassured me that she would handle all of this and told me to rest easy. I tried. I stayed in my room for a good, long time.

Mom handled everything in her usual strong and determined manner. Everything included calling Pastor Sorenson to tell him this quickly planned marriage was now off and calling Jody, D, and Kay to ask them to spread the word that Patty's wedding had been canceled and that Patty was not available to see or talk to anyone, just in case any of them tried to stop by or call me. She said I wasn't to be disturbed because I needed to rest, which was probably true, even though all I had done for a week was sleep, eat, and sleep some more. The only person Mom failed to contact was Gene himself. She later told me that she had tried a hundred times to call him, but that his phone was busy every time she called. Otherwise, Mom had once again handled everything to her satisfaction.

*****

Afterwards, I heard through the grapevine that about forty of Gene's family and friends, along with about fifteen of my friends (who had not gotten word), showed up at the Lutheran Church on

Highway 61 and watched as Gene stood at the altar and waited for his bride to walk down that aisle. She never came, and as they waited and waited, they watched the tears start to flow from dear Gene's eyes. Eventually, he gave up and allowed himself to be consoled by his mom and siblings as they led him out the doors of the church and back to their house in St. Paul.

Gene left for Midway Island a week later and remained in the Navy for the next twenty-five years, ever the good sailor. Much later, I learned that on his next leave, he stopped in San Francisco and met and married a pretty, young blonde, about five foot four, a neat size eight. I was happy to know that he had found the right woman this time and had gone on to live a good life. Although I felt bad for jilting him at the altar, I also knew deep down that if we had married, it would most likely not have worked out. It was a strong feeling deep inside me. And, I didn't want anyone left heartbroken, not Gene and not me. So in the end, we were both lucky that I had realized, before it was too late, that I had been more in love with love and adventure and not yet ready to leave my home of White Bear Lake.

PART VII
TEARS AND CHEERS

The Phone Call

I knew my father's name was Nick, but I had never seen him or talked with him. I would stare at him from behind the curtains when he came to pick up my brothers for their scheduled monthly visits, and would see him waving at the shy face peeking out from the window, but we never met each other face to face. Then one day the phone rang. This phone call broke my world wide open.

After the whirlwind Gene fiasco, I knew it was time for me to be on my own. I figured I had put Mom through enough already, so I moved out of her house and into a little place on Elk Drive. On the morning of the phone call, I had just finished my breakfast when the kitchen phone rang. Wondering who would be calling me so early, I picked up the receiver and said, "Hello?"

An unfamiliar voice on the other end asked, "Is this Patty?"

"This is Patty," I said. "Who is this?"

The rather gruff yet pleasant voice replied, "This is your dad."

I nearly dropped the phone and fell on the floor. I said, "That can't be. Prove it." As hot tears started running down my cheeks, I grabbed a kitchen chair to sit on. I was in total shock and disbelief. I thought this had to be a prank call from a crazy person.

The voice on the other end spoke with obvious self-assurance. "Sweetheart, this is Nick, your father."

I challenged him again. "Who's my Mom?" I asked. "What's her name? What's my middle name? Where does she live? What is the street? What are my brothers' names? When was I born?"

He answered all my questions without hesitation. "Your Mom is Ruth. Your middle name is Ann, and your oldest brother is Mel and the other is John." While he answered the rest, I began shaking uncontrollably. "Why are you calling me, now?" I demanded, with a mixture of curiosity and rage.

"What do you want?" I continued. "You never called me or showed any interest in seeing me, ever!"

Then he said, "Patty, your Mom never allowed me to see you. That's why I have never called before.

"She hates me to this day, but I have always loved you and always wanted you to visit with your brothers when they came for their one weekend a month. Believe me! I tried and tried to get your mom to soften and agree to that, but she said always said, 'No way!' She called me a sorry-ass drunk and was afraid that I would hurt you. You must know that I would never hurt you, never, and that I love you very much."

My face was soaked with tears. I said, "Come see me. Where are you calling from? Are you close by? Do you know that I have my own little house that I rent? I'm working at the Target in Maplewood, too. Did you know that?"

"Yes," he said. "Your brother Mel tells me everything about you. I always ask him how you're doing.

"You must be beautiful with that golden-blonde hair. You were such a beautiful baby."

"You saw me as a baby? When? I thought Mom never let you near me," I said, my mind swirling with all this new information.

"I went to the hospital when you were in the nursery and asked the nurse which baby was Patricia Ann. She pointed you out and even let me hold you. I loved you from the start and have loved you all my life, more than you will ever know. Did you know you have my eyes?"

"Come see me," I said. "Let's go to lunch or dinner. Can you?"

Nick said, "Yes, sweetie, now that I have your number, I will call you again and we will have lunch, dinner, or whatever you want. I promise." At that, I asked him, "How did you get my number? It's not listed in the phone book."

"Mel gave it to me," he said. "I called him yesterday for it." I then asked, "What is your number?" I heard an audible sigh before he answered me again. "Patty, I'm calling from a phone booth. My phone at home doesn't work right now." I believed him. I believed everything he was telling me.

Sometimes phone lines go down and that is why there are phone booths. It never occurred to me that there could be any other reason for a phone not working.

We continued to talk for several more minutes. My dad—Nick, the man Mom hated—went on to tell me about his brother, my Uncle Eugene, whom I had never met. He said that they had always been best friends and that he had learned a few days ago that his brother was now in the hospital dying of cirrhosis of the liver. Dad said, "It's not looking good for him. I'm so worried that I will lose my best friend in life." I said, "I am so sorry to hear this. Is he your older or younger brother?" Dad replied, "Older by two years." Then he turned his thoughts back to me and asked, "Patty, do you need anything? Money? Anything?"

"If you want, I always need money," I said. "I pay my own way for everything. I don't ask Mom for anything because she only has enough to get by, so a little extra every now and then would be helpful."

He asked for my address, and I gave it to him, but not before I asked, "Are you sure? Are you sure you can help me with some money?" Dad answered, "Yes, honey, I will send you some money today. I feel badly that we have never had a chance to get to know each other. Please let me do this one thing for you." "Sure, Dad, that would help me a lot."

The conversation ended with him telling me that he had always loved me, and by now, I felt the same and told him so. I said, "Call me anytime. Take care of yourself, and I hope Uncle Eugene pulls through."

Dad answered, "Patty, thank you, so much. I'll stay in touch. I promise."

I hung up the phone feeling as if I had just awakened from a dream. Had this really happened? Had I really just talked with my father—the father I had never known—for half an hour?

Wow! I couldn't believe what I had just heard or what I was feeling about this phone call. I'd been shaken to my core. I couldn't stop crying, so I wandered in the field behind my house for what seemed like hours, trying to make sense of this bizarre experience. Why? Why had he called me? Why had he called now, after all these years? I didn't have any answers. I only knew that his call had changed my feelings toward my father. My father did love me, had always loved me, and now I knew it was true. It was no longer just a wish I had held onto as a child. By the end of the day, I was smiling and hoping he would call again soon.

I would always love my father for making this phone call. He had changed my life forever.

The Funeral

A couple of weeks after the phone call, Mom mentioned that she had heard that Nick's brother Eugene had passed away from liver disease. "Damn fool, wouldn't give up the booze for nothing. See what happened. It killed him. It'll probably kill that bastard Nick, too."

I just listened to her vent and never mentioned a word about the phone call. I didn't want her to know I had talked with my father. Never. It was my prized secret. I did tell Mel, though, and thanked him for giving Dad my number. Mel said that Dad had always wanted to get to know me and that he had been sober for the last month or so because of his concern for his brother's health.

A week later, a check for five hundred dollars arrived in the mail with a tiny note that said, "To you, my beautiful Patty. I love you. I hope this will help with your rent." Again, I welled up with tears as I walked back up the driveway to my little house on Elk Drive. Life could not have been sweeter.

Four months later, however, Mom got word that Dad was in the hospital with cirrhosis of the liver.

Mel, Johnny, and I were standing in the kitchen when Mel said, "Mom, Johnny and I are going over to Ramsey County Hospital right now; let Patty come with us."

Mom snapped back, "Go ahead. Go see what alcohol does to you. Maybe you all will learn from this. As far as I'm concerned, it's good riddance to him."

"Thank you, Mom," I whispered as I hurried to catch up with the boys.

I hadn't been in a hospital since my days as a candy striper, but I immediately recalled the pungent smells of antiseptic, urine, and lingering illness that permeated the air. Dad's room was empty of flowers, but there were a couple of get-well cards on the bedside table. His face and stomach were swollen, and his color was yellow. A nurse said it was jaundice. I didn't know what that meant.

The nurse said he was dying, and then she left us alone with him. He couldn't speak, yet he looked at each of us in a most endearing way that told us he loved us all dearly. Mel tried to feed him some cherry Jell-O (I guess everyone in hospitals is served Jell-O), and he slowly opened his mouth to take it. Johnny turned away, crying. He couldn't watch. As Dad finished the small bowl of Jell-O, I saw some of it dripping out of the corner of his mouth and running down his chin. I grabbed a tissue and wiped his face. He gave me a gentle smile. His eyes seemed to beam from deep inside him. I cried.

We stayed for an hour or so and promised we'd return tomorrow. He gave us a gentle, tender wave goodbye. We couldn't make it to the hospital the next day or the next because Mel had to work and he was the only one with a car. Three days later, Mel heard that Dad had been released from the hospital and was back home again. Evidently, Eugene's wife had agreed to care for him, and he was gradually getting better.

That's good news, I thought. Maybe he'll call again soon.

I waited and hoped, but there were no more phone calls from Dad. I later learned that as soon as he was released from the hospital, he had started drinking again … heavily … every day.

*****

Two months later, I received word that there had been a fire at Dad's house. The story was that he had been sitting in his living room on the couch, directly across from the wall heater. The old heater, which probably hadn't been serviced in years, exploded, bursting into flames. A neighbor must have heard the loud boom and called the police. The fire department came within minutes, but it was too late.

They found his body burning on the throw rug in front of the couch. They said he had died within seconds. A ring on his finger and the watch on his wrist had melted into his skin. The first one notified was Eugene's wife, who lived just two houses down. She called Mel. I got the awful news later that day.

The funeral was three days later. There would be a closed-casket wake at Eugene's home first, before Dad's burial in the Polish Cemetery of New Brighton. Mom said I could attend with my brothers, but I would have gone with or without her permission. For the first time in my life, I was about to meet all my aunts, uncles, and cousins from Dad's side of the family. At first, surrounded by all these strangers, I felt shy and timid, like an outsider who shouldn't be there, but the sadness that everyone felt about the loss of my father overcame any fears I had about not belonging. I was repeatedly introduced to everyone as Nick's only daughter, the baby, and everyone seemed genuinely happy to meet me. Looking around the room, these new relatives, although sad, all looked well dressed; the women wore silky flowing black dresses and the low kind of high heels that older women usually wear. The men were in, what appeared to me, TV gangster-like three-piece, pinstriped black or navy blue suits—with slicked-back, black wavy hair, just like my dad's. They all seemed nice and friendly.

At some point, two sweet, gray-haired ladies came up to me and gave me a huge hug. "So you're Patty," the one said. "We've heard all about you, and you are just as adorable as he said you were.

"You have your daddy's eyes, you know. How old are you, sweetheart?"

"I'm almost nineteen," I said. "Are you his sisters?" The shorter, rather pudgy one said, "Yes. I'm Donna, and this is Doris." Doris then said, "Your dad often spoke of you." "That is, when he was sober," interrupted Donna. "It's too bad he let the liquor take him away from you. That wall heater should have been replaced years ago. The damn fool!" she said, with tears running down her face. "Damn fool!" echoed Doris.

Yes, I thought, he had been a damn fool, which were kinder words than Mom had called him. He had died because he had neglected to have the heater repaired, but I had a nagging suspicion that Mom may have been right about the liquor. No doubt, it had killed him, just as it had killed his brother, poisoning his insides one drink at a time. However, my underlying anger was overtaken by the deep sadness of losing a father I had never known, a man who, everyone at the funeral told me, loved to laugh, loved his family, but mostly loved to drink with his brother Eugene.

As Polish people do (so I was learning), we went to the cemetery for the burial service and then onto his favorite bar in

New Brighton. There sat all his other favorite friends, who had spent many a day, week, and year on those bar stools, drinking away their sorrows and regrets. We ate Polish food and drank to my dad. The party continued with a Polka dance (with band) that lasted through the night. We didn't get home until around one in the morning.

The memory of Dad's memorial service has remained with me forever. We celebrated his life in the best way possible. I had lost my dad, but I had gained an abundance of aunts, uncles, and cousins.

They say you can't miss what you never had, but I'm not so sure that's true. Dad was just forty-nine years old.

PART VIII
ADVENTURES TO COME MY WAY

Leaving White Bear Lake

"Hurry up, Patty," Mom called from the driveway. "We're ready to leave. Gather up your things and get in the RV. Your boxes are already in the back of the truck. If you need anything else after you get there, we'll either ship it to you or bring it with us on our next trip."

"Be there in a minute," I yelled from my basement bedroom, throwing the last of my stuff into my travel bag. It was time for me to say good-bye to White Bear—no looking back, no regrets.

No doubt, I would miss the fun of ice skating and sledding down the bluffs of the upper St. Croix River at Grandpa's house, or picnicking on the lake in sub-zero temperatures with the Looney Latooneys. There would be none of that where I was headed, but that was okay with me. I was ready to start a new life in a new environment that promised year-round sunshine and warm temperatures, not to mention new friends, new opportunities, and new adventures.

Actually, I was more than ready. Since moving to White Bear in the third grade, I had suffered through and survived enough drama and trauma to last a lifetime. At times, it was all too painful to think about, but I knew I would never forget these events and people. However, at this point in my life, I needed to make a clean break. I had hoped to go to San Francisco. That had been my friend Jean's dream, and my grandmother's favorite vacation destination. The mural on her dining room wall had fascinated me since childhood, and I had promised myself I would go there, too—someday. Unfortunately, I wouldn't get there this trip. We were heading for the Southwest; we being me, Mom, Howie, and the family pet, an apricot poodle named Caesar, who went everywhere with Mom and Howie in their RV. I was the tag-along hitchhiker on this trip.

Every year as the weather in Minnesota, and all of the north, turned mean and ugly, Mom and Howie made a winter get-away trip to warmer climes. This year, they had decided to spend a month basking in the heat of the Arizona desert. Since they were headed that way anyway, they agreed to give me a lift to Phoenix, where I had made arrangements to move in with Bonnie, a high school friend who had relocated six months prior and had a good job at the U-Haul franchise in downtown Phoenix. She had promised me, "Life is sweet here in the Southwest." Sounded good to me. Sounded good to Mom and Howie, too. They had already done enough damage control on my behalf, especially after my embarrassing cold-feet wedding escape from Navy-man Gene, the groom of Mom's dreams.

"Patty! You better get your ass out here, or you're gonna be left behind," Mom's voice boomed again, a little louder this time.

"I'm coming. I'm coming!" I shouted as I took one last look around the little green rambler on Floral Drive. I guess I was trying to capture a few indelible images to etch into my FMB, otherwise known as my "forever memory bank." I peeked into the corner bedroom that had been mine when we moved in the house. It belonged to Kris now, and my exuberant orange walls had been repainted, much to my dismay, a dainty pink. Walking through the kitchen, I couldn't help but notice that Mom's prized black-and-white Formica table with the red vinyl chairs, once so bright and shiny new, had been worn down to dull shades of gray and muddy maroon, no doubt the result of all those family suppers at six and lingering conversations over steaming mugs of hot coffee.

Running through the kitchen door, I made a quick detour to the backyard. I had to say good-bye to my lovely willow tree. The little sapling branch that I had plucked, planted, and tended with such hope and love was now as tall as the house. It seemed to sense my imminent departure, because although there wasn't even a mere whisper of a breeze, its trailing branches waved softly, as if wishing me a fond farewell.

"*Patty!* Where the hell are you? We're leaving, *now!*" Mom again, and this time she meant business.

Running around the side of the house, I managed to give a quick hug and kiss to Loretta and D, who had come to see me off, and then literally jumped into the RV as Howie started pulling truck and trailer out of the driveway. I didn't know what adventures lay ahead, but it didn't matter. After growing up in White Bear Lake, I knew I was ready for anything life could throw at me. For sure, life hadn't always been easy, but beyond a doubt, White Bear Lake had been a great place to call home.

Epilogue

The dreadful disease, Alzheimer's, claimed my mother's life a few years ago. Even though she regularly took the Lord's name in vain when my brothers and I were growing up, I know in my heart that she is now in heaven with her father and all the people who treated her nicely throughout her life, including Howie, who passed shortly after her. Cussing only occurs "once in a blue moon" in my home and only on the rare occasions that really warrant "a blue streak," but I credit my dear mom each and every time I need to use her language. I also believe that dancing is probably a standard event in heaven, since there's no need to wait for Lawrence Welk or the weekend to practice the polka!

Pink Cadillac's still get my attention when I see one, even though I know Bruce is long gone from this earth, too. Likewise, per Grandma's instruction, I have never touched a Lady Slipper plant, but now that I think about it, I haven't seen one anywhere since I moved to the Southwest. My lovely little willow branch, which I planted and tended with such care, grew to be a healthy, towering tree. It still draws attention from passersby because it remains the largest tree on the corner of Floral Drive. Because I still have a bad reaction to hornet stings (and get stung, on average, once per summer), I keep Benadryl on hand at all times! Oh, and by the way, swimming naked is still the way to go whenever and wherever possible. Trust me. I've never been arrested for skinny-dipping (or anything else for that matter) since leaving White Bear.

About ten years ago, Gene, the jilted sailor, found me via the internet and sent me the nicest letter. He explained that he had forgiven me, had often thought of me, and wanted me to know that soon after he returned to duty in California, he met a young girl with long blonde hair and he married her; they had stayed married all these years. He said he still rode a Harley, which really impressed me. I replied that I, too, had finally married, but not to a sailor or Harley kind of guy. I told him how pleased I was that he had reached out to locate me and that I was sorry to have left him at the altar all those years ago. We didn't get to kiss, but we did make up and have remained email buddies ever since.

Also, via Facebook and email, I have remained in contact with one of those lovely aunties I met at my father's funeral. Through this connection, I have been able to put more of the missing pieces together about that side of my family and my Polish heritage. To her, I shall be forever grateful.

Sadly, Paco, my childhood boy friend, passed away last year after living with Parkinson's disease for many years. My heart still aches to receive one of his periodic phone calls; he had the best laugh in the entire world and was a true friend and confidant. We shared conversations that I could have had with no other human. God willing, someday I will see him, and Jean, and Kay, and all those who have gone on before to wait for me in that heavenly place. Until then, their stories will live on in my heart and through the pages of this book, and the dancing will waltz on.